SANDMAN

SANDMAN

DAVID HODGES

ROBERT HALE · LONDON

© David Hodges 2015
First published in Great Britain 2015

ISBN 978-0-7198-1835-6

Robert Hale Limited
Clerkenwell House
Clerkenwell Green
London EC1R 0HT

www.halebooks.com

2 4 6 8 10 9 7 5 3 1

Typeset in New Century Schoolbook
Printed and bound in Great Britain by
Berforts Information Press Ltd

DEDICATION

This book is dedicated to my wife, Elizabeth, for all her love, patience and support over so many wonderful years. Also to my late mother and father, whose faith in my ambition to become a writer remained steadfast throughout their lifetime, and whose tragic passing has left a hole in my life that will never be filled.

AUTHOR'S NOTE

ALTHOUGH THE ACTION in this novel is set in the Avon and Somerset police area, the story itself and all the characters in it are entirely fictitious. Similarly, at the time of writing, there is no police station in Highbridge – this has been drawn entirely from the author's imagination to ensure no connection is made between any existing police station or personnel in the force and the content of this novel. Furthermore, some poetic licence has been used in relation to the local police hierarchy and structure, and some of the specific procedures followed by Avon and Somerset police in order to meet the requirements of the plot. Nevertheless, the policing background depicted in the novel is broadly in accord with the national picture and these little departures from fact will, hopefully, not spoil the reading enjoyment of serving or retired police officers for whom I have the utmost respect.

I would particularly like to stress that, although the nightmare flooding scenario, which forms the background to my novel, did take place on the Somerset Levels in the winter of 2014 – with tragic devastating consequences for this beautiful part of the world and so many of its inhabitants – the hilltop village of Lowmoor, as depicted in the story, is purely fictitious.

I would like to add my sincere admiration for the people of the Somerset Levels, whose courage and vibrant community spirit during the long months that their homes and businesses were overwhelmed by the waters is a lesson to us all.

David Hodges

BEFORE THE FACT

February 2014

RAIN. COLD, HEAVY, unstoppable and virtually continuous for the past six weeks. Some weather experts cited climate change; others said it was just a cyclical process that occurred naturally, while many of the locals were convinced it was due to poor maintenance of the river system. All seemed agreed, though, that the series of powerful storms that had ripped through the south and south-west of England – piling momentous waves over the sea walls and flooding vast tracts of the countryside – were the worst for 250 years.

The patchwork of fields making up the bulk of the wild Somerset Levels were beyond saturation point; they bled into overfull rhynes that in turn were trying to discharge their loads into rivers already bursting their banks. Inland lakes formed which were only separated in places by fast disappearing hedgerows and grass strips. Combined with high spring tides and whipped up by seventy to eighty mph winds, the swollen waters developed a terrifying ferocity all of their own, engulfing roads and flooding low-level farms and other properties with impunity.

On the higher ground, the elfin lights of the small village of Lowmoor flickered in the deluge as sheets of water cascaded from the rooftop gutters of the cottages, creeping up the slope towards the local inn and, just beyond it, the ancient

Norman church that, despite the rain, found itself bathed in the eerie white light of a smoky moon. Marooned by the still rising waters and now accessible only by boat or helicopter, it seemed to the hundred or so inhabitants as if they had been returned to the Dark Ages, virtually abandoned by the rest of mankind, like the poor wretches of a leper colony or a community struck down by bubonic plague.

The girl in the green anorak was scared – very scared – and it had nothing to do with the weather. She had missed the late afternoon boat service that had been set up by volunteers to enable villagers to get to shops, schools and work places and she had stupidly not thought to arrange for the local man whom she had persuaded to ferry her to the isolated village in the first place to return for her. Now she was stranded until the regular morning boat arrived at around ten – and, with telephone lines to the village down and her mobile phone dropped somewhere when she had fled, she had no means of contacting anyone. Standing at the end of the street, staring at the water lapping her booted feet, she shivered as the wind moaned over the flooded Levels. It plucked at her clothes and drove the rain into her face inside the anorak's hood with painful force; the water bouncing off the bare skin of her thigh where she had cut herself on some barbed wire on a wall she had had to climb over. Only the cold had reduced the pain, but she could still feel the wound throbbing and she knew the bleeding hadn't stopped. What a mess!

She had contemplated trying to wade through the water, between the twin lines of hedgerows that marked what had once been the main road in and out of the village – such was her desperation – but common sense had prevailed. She had been told earlier that the water was at least four feet deep and she could see in the way it swirled and twisted in the moonlight that it held a deadly strength which would sweep her away before she had gone even a few feet. Furthermore, the hedgerows bordering the edges of the road disappeared in places along its length, which meant that it was virtually impossible at times, even in broad daylight, to see where the road ended and the fields began, let alone trying to do so on a rainy night.

She knew *they* would be out looking for her by now and turned to stare back up the street through the sheets of water being jettisoned from the gutters of the cottages, but she saw no one. They would be expecting her to hide somewhere in the house or its grounds and would be checking all the usual places, but when they came up with nothing, they would start thinking about the village outside and then it would only be a matter of time before they found her – even in this weather.

She had to find a secure hiding place – somewhere they would never think of looking, but where? She was effectively on an 'island', a few acres consisting of a dozen cottages, a church, a pub, a small shop and a farm. There were some fields, of course, and a copse, but she didn't fancy spending the night out in the open. The farm had a couple of barns but that was the first place they would look and, as the farmer had already given up and left after moving his herd out, who would be there to stop them? As for the pub, in the absence of evening customers, that had now closed and was battened down against the wind, so she would get no help there. Then she thought of the church, the ancient rambling building with its bell tower, crypt and sacristy. That might be a possibility, but she would have to hurry; her pursuers were probably already out in the rain looking for her even as she thought about it.

Swinging round, she pulled her hood tighter about her face with one hand and ducked her head against the rain as the wind slammed into her from behind like a giant's massive fist.

The gate into the churchyard was wide open, blown back by the force of the wind, with the bottom corner jammed into the sodden grass. The gravestones stood out in the moonlight, crooked broken teeth grinning obscenely as she ran along the gravel path to the porch, praying that the double doors would prove to be unlocked.

There was a latch on the right-hand door and it cracked like a pistol shot, raising hollow echoes in the vaulted interior. The door itself opened quietly enough when she pushed it open, however, and she peered into a heavy gloom only partially relieved by the moonlight streaming through the big rose window above the altar.

The place appeared deserted, but she stiffened involuntarily as the building trembled slightly under a sudden gust of the powerful buffeting wind. Pulling a small torch from her pocket, she switched it on to probe the shadows where the moonlight failed to reach and made a slow hesitant approach along the nave towards the chancel, her footsteps ringing on the stone-slabbed floor. At first she saw only lines of pews and the stone busts of medieval figures peering at her from high in the vaulted roof but then, entering the chancel, which was separated from the main body of the church by a carved wooden screen, her gaze fell on a low-level door set deep in the stone wall to one side. The crypt? It had to be and it was as good a place to hide as any. Turning sharply to head through the choir stalls towards it, she bent down and twisted the ancient iron ring that served as a handle, praying that the door would prove to be unlocked.

And she was in luck. There was a loud 'crack' and it swung inwards on creaking hinges, releasing a blast of cold stale air. The beam of her torch revealed a narrow stone staircase dropping away before her and she breathed a sigh of relief – somewhere to hide. But that relief soon turned out to be premature. Following the stone steps down into the darkness, she caught the gleam of water as she rounded a curve in the wall, just feet from the bottom, and moments later the steps came to an abrupt halt.

Moonlight probed the subterranean vault through small,

square iron gratings set in the floor of the church above and she didn't need a torch to tell her that the crypt was flooded, maybe to a depth of several feet. The central stone pillars marched away in the light like ghostly white sentinels and the lids of the stone sarcophagi were only just visible above the gently eddying water which continued to seep through holes and cracks in the foundations from the waterlogged earth.

Muttering an oath, she turned quickly and headed back up the steps, her mind in overdrive. There was no time to look for another hiding place outside the church. She had to find somewhere else within the building and quickly. Even now one of *them* could be walking through the gate and up the path. The west tower. That was her only real alternative. She could hide in the bell chamber, concealed behind one of those massive bells, but first she had to see if the door to the tower was unlocked, like the crypt.

As it turned out, however, she never got the chance to find out. The grating sound of the crypt door being pulled open was followed by heavy footsteps on the steps above her and, even as she froze where she stood, extinguishing her torch, another more powerful torch probed the darkness around the curve of the wall that temporarily shielded the new arrival from view. She was trapped.

CHAPTER 1

DETECTIVE INSPECTOR TED ROSCOE was a committed cynic. The job and a failed marriage had done that to him. Twenty-eight years at the sharp end of police work, dealing with murderers, drug addicts, armed robbers and paedophiles – including ten years of marriage to a wife who had humiliated him by leaving him for another woman – had not blessed the balding ex-Royal Marine with a sunny trusting disposition or a favourable impression of his fellow man – or woman for that matter. The scowl that was etched into his slab-like features when he stomped into the CID office in Avon and Somerset's Highbridge police station was certainly not indicative of someone with a sunny outlook either and Detective Sergeant Kate Lewis looked up from the file on her desk with a wary frown as the office door gave way under the force of his heavy muscular frame.

'Guv,' she acknowledged, smoothing her shoulder-length auburn hair back from her pretty freckled face and climbing to her feet. 'Coffee?'

'Where is everybody?' he demanded, noting, as his dark boot-button eyes swept round the room, that she was the only one there. 'On bloody strike?'

She sighed and swung away from her computer screen to face him. 'Both Jamie Foster and Fred Alloway are out dealing with the theft of diesel from a couple of farms on the Levels, Guv,' she said. 'Seems we have some nasty arseholes taking advantage of the flooding to carry out raids on abandoned properties.'

He grunted. 'What about your other half?' he sniped. 'At home, with his pinny on, doing the washing up, is he?'

There was a flash of irritation in her blue eyes as she crossed to the coffee machine in the corner. She was well used to her boss's caustic, intimidating manner and his frequent derogatory comments about her husband but they still got to her. '*Hayden* is actually dealing with a misper inquiry,' she said tightly. 'Has been since he came on this morning.'

He grunted, raising an eyebrow. 'So, what does he want – a bloody medal?' he growled, then added almost as an afterthought, 'What misper?'

Kate poured him a mug of black coffee and turned to hand it to him before returning to her desk and settling herself on one corner with her ankles crossed. 'Woman journalist – Ellie Landy – missing from her digs in Highbridge. According to her landlady, who reported her missing, she left the place three days ago to go off somewhere and never came back.'

Roscoe slipped a wad of chewing gum in his mouth and began chewing furiously as he digested the information. 'Journalist? How old?'

'Twenty-one, I believe.'

'Twenty-one?' he echoed and, to Kate's incredulity, managed to take a gulp of his coffee without swallowing the gum. 'Not a juvenile then, so why are we wasting time on her? She's probably over the side with some local hunk.'

'For three days?'

He shrugged. 'It happens.' He grinned. 'Maybe she decided on an extra-long lie-in.'

Kate gave him an old-fashioned look, wincing as he blew a large bubble with his gum, then sucked it back in, leaving a grey trace attached to the underside of his Stalin-like moustache.

'We still have to make inquiries,' she went on. 'She could

16

have fallen foul of the flooding and drowned. Some places are under six to eight feet of water.'

He snorted. 'Yeah, and she could have just done a bunk to avoid paying the bill – or even been abducted by the bloody tooth fairy!' He waved an arm dismissively as he turned towards his office at the end of the room. 'Get the control room to call up that "missing link" of yours and tell him not to make a meal of it – I've got his soddin' annual appraisal to do yet.'

Kate made a sour grimace, straightening and reaching back across her desk for the phone. But she never got to ring the control room; they rang her even as her hand closed on the receiver.

The conversation with the operator was short – and anything but sweet – and Kate's freckled face was grim as she set the phone down and crossed the room to Roscoe's office.

He looked up quickly when she entered after a peremptory knock and his eyes narrowed as he read the expression on her face.

'Problem?' he snapped.

She nodded. 'Sus death on the Levels.'

'Sus?'

'Woman found wedged amongst some driftwood in the River Parrett.'

'And?' he queried, sensing that there was more.

'ID card on the corpse suggests she's a journalist named Ellie Landy.'

'Shit!' he breathed.

Kate treated him to a tight ironic smile. 'No sign of the tooth fairy, though, Guv,' she added with just a hint of malice. 'Perhaps *she's* the one having a lie-in.'

Hayden Lewis looked hot and flustered when he stumbled into the small pumping station, which clung to a spit of land just above the flooded landscape, and it was evident that he had raced to the scene as soon as he'd been told about the dead woman. His green Parka was undone to reveal a badly creased pink shirt that hadn't been tucked into his trousers properly and the rain had plastered his mop of untidy fair hair to his head like a miniature wet haystack. For ever seen as a look-alike of the Mayor of London, Boris Johnson, on this occasion he looked more like a refugee from the twilight world of the meths drinker and Kate closed her eyes briefly in resignation as he stood there gaping inanely at the corpse of the young woman in the green anorak stretched out on the floor on a tarpaulin the other side of a line of blue and white police tape.

Kate took a deep breath. 'Ellie Landy by the look of it,' she said tightly before he asked the inevitable question. 'Uniform found her press ID card in a coat pocket with her wallet.'

Hayden nodded, but avoided meeting her gaze. 'Darned shame,' he mumbled.

Roscoe studied him narrowly and slipped a wad of chewing gum into his mouth. 'Oh it's that all right,' he growled. 'So, what do we know about her?'

Hayden looked puzzled. 'Know?'

'Well, you were following up the misper inquiry, weren't you?'

Hayden abruptly cottoned on and nodded again. 'Oh that, yes. Not much joy at present, sir.' He cleared his throat. 'It's likely she was down here reporting on the flooding.'

'What a surprise, Sherlock. Like half the bloody media, I would think. What paper was she with?'

'Not sure yet.'

Roscoe studied at him, chewing slowly. 'Don't know much, do you?'

'Working on it, sir.'

Roscoe's gaze lingered for a few seconds. 'Then you'd better work a bloody sight harder, Lewis, hadn't you?' he snapped.

'I think she was with some London news agency, sir,' the uniformed sergeant standing just behind Roscoe cut in.

'There were half a dozen business cards in the wallet in her anorak, but I didn't make a note of the name. The wallet's in my car, if you want me to check?'

The DI dismissed the offer with a wave of his hand but half-turned towards him. 'Anything else?'

The skipper shook his head and Roscoe frowned. 'Mobile? Notebook? Anything like that?'

'Not that we could find, sir, though we didn't conduct a thorough search – thought it best to wait until the pathologist had taken a look at her first – but maybe she wasn't working at the time.'

'Maybe,' Kate cut in, 'but I can't see a journalist going any-where without a mobile, even if she left her notebook at home.'

'Perhaps she was using the mobile when she fell in the river?' the sergeant suggested.

Roscoe emitted a non-committal grunt, then turned back to the corpse as the portly man in the protective overalls straightened up from his crouched position beside it, panting heavily.

'Looks like a classic case of drowning anyway,' forensic pathologist, Gerry Stone, announced, his pink perspiring cheeks creased into a beaming smile.

'Time of death?' Roscoe barked back, shelving his gum in the side of his mouth for a moment.

Stone pulled off his hood and thought for a moment. 'I'd say she's been in the water at least a couple of days. Quite a bit of gas is evident in the body, which is undoubtedly what brought her to the surface and, though the low temperature will to some extent have delayed the progressive maceration of the skin I would be looking for in a twenty-four to thirty-six hour immersion, the initial signs are still present – blanched colour, swelling and wrinkling of the finger-tips—'

'Yeah, yeah, yeah,' Roscoe cut in quickly, as usual, intoler-ant of clinical explanations and keen to cut to the chase. 'So, accidental death then?'

The pathologist frowned. 'Oh, I think you're jumping the gun there, Detective Inspector,' he admonished. 'I'm merely saying that, from my initial observations of the condition of the body, it seems likely that she drowned. I can find no obvious signs of violence, apart from some superficial cuts, bruising and abrasions on her hands, face and head, and some tears to her fingernails. I would suggest these were probably sustained after death when her body came into contact with the river bottom or floating debris – not unusual in a drowning case – and, with the river now double its size after bursting its banks, she could have struck anything, from submerged fence posts to brick walls. Nothing really sinister, though. She's also plainly taken in a lot of water, which suggests that her respiratory system was still functioning immediately prior to her death, but I won't be able to say much more—'

'Until after the PM,' Roscoe finished for him, well used to the familiar stock phrase used by almost every forensic pathologist he had encountered in his long career.

Stone shrugged. 'That's about it,' he replied. 'I'm minded to take some river samples to see if we can match them with the water she has absorbed. That would serve to confirm or otherwise the location of her death, but apart from this, there's not a lot more I can do here. We'll just have to see what the PM can tell us.'

The DI grunted. 'Very little, I bet,' he grumbled. 'Bloody river has seen to that.' He resumed chewing. 'Keep me informed of anything you turn up, though.'

'You'll be the first to know,' Stone said and made a vain attempt at humour by raising three podgy fingers of one hand close together in an erect salute. 'Scout's honour.'

Roscoe was not amused and ignored his witticism, his teeth chomping noisily on his gum. 'And you're sure we have no idea where she actually went in?' he growled, half-turning towards the uniform sergeant who had remained at his elbow.

The sergeant shook his head. 'No idea at all, sir,' he confirmed. 'The body could have been swept down here for quite a distance before it got stuck in some driftwood. Current is very strong – especially now that the river is so swollen.'

The DI blew a bubble with his gum. 'So, who pulled her out?' he queried.

'Bloke from the Environment Agency – a Gus Hand. He came to check on the station pump and saw her body caught up in the flotsam just below the pumping station. Said she definitely wasn't there when he came by here yesterday.'

'But there's nothing to say she couldn't have been dumped here after he left?'

'Not if my assessment is correct, Mr Roscoe,' the pathologist put in a little indignantly. 'This isn't a corpse that has been "dumped" in the river overnight. She has been under water for quite some time before surfacing and becoming trapped here.'

Roscoe grunted an acknowledgment, but continued to address the sergeant. 'Where is this Gus Hand now?'

'Out checking on other pumps.' The uniformed man tensed when he saw Roscoe's scowl deepen and, perhaps anticipating a criticism, he added quickly, 'He was interviewed, sir,' he said, 'but was adamant that he saw no one at the scene or anywhere near it and had never clapped eyes on the dead woman before. One of my lads noted his address and took a quick statement off him – just in case we needed to see him again.'

The DI nodded, apparently satisfied, and turned towards the door. 'Looks like just another straightforward drowning then,' he commented. 'Silly bitch probably got too close to the edge somewhere and fell in.'

Kate winced at his blatant insensitivity, but, knowing from past experience that it would be a waste of time trying to pull him up on it, she simply followed him outside without commenting on the remark. 'We'll need to get hold of a relative for

ID purposes,' she said instead, stopping by his car.

He nodded. 'OK, I'll leave that with you, but I don't intend going overboard with what looks to me like a straightforward accidental drowning. Just go through the usual motions, eh? I've already got SOCO en route, just to keep everyone happy, even though there's not much they can do here under the circumstances, and when they've done their bit, we'll get the stiff off to the morgue.' He snapped his fingers. 'Oh, yeah, and tell that bright spark of yours back there to come and see me for his appraisal at 1500 hours this afternoon. Might as well get that crap over today anyway.' He bared his teeth in the semblance of a grin as he threw open the door of his car and slid behind the wheel. 'You can come back in his motor once you've tied everything up here, but no games of mothers and fathers on the way, eh?'

Kate met his gaze with an icy stare, closing the door behind him and standing back as he started the engine. 'Anything else, sir?' she snapped through the open window.

His grin broadened. 'No, I think I've covered about every-thing, don't you?' he shouted, noisily engaging first gear.

'Too bloody much,' she murmured as he drove away.

As it transpired, SOCO – or the Scientific Investigation team as they now liked to be called – didn't arrive on the scene until half an hour after Roscoe had left and Kate used the wait to put her husband straight on one or two things as they sat in his CID car.

'Dipstick!' she snapped as an opener. 'Why the hell do you do it?'

Hayden seemed taken aback. 'Why do I do what, old girl?'

'Well, for starters, turn up here looking like a bundle of shit!'

He made a pained grimace. 'Oh thanks for the vote of con-fidence – and in such colourful language too.'

She stared at him incredulously. 'You have the cheek to

censure me for using bad language after your performance this morning? Do you realize I had to cover for you with Roscoe – yet again?'

He winced, looking uncomfortable. 'Sorry, old girl?'

'And don't call me old girl, not when we're on duty!'

He gave a sheepish grin. 'Sorry – *Sergeant*.'

She controlled herself with an effort. 'Listen to me, you useless prat, I told Roscoe you were out on the Landy misper inquiry when he walked into the office this morning—'

'Well, I was, in a manner of speaking.'

'Only after I rang home to get you out of bed. Must you always be bloody late?'

He flinched. 'I find getting up early a bit of a problem, you know that.'

'Early?' she blazed. 'When I left you this morning, it was after eight o'clock and you promised me you would be in the nick by nine, as rostered.' He didn't answer and she studied him suspiciously for a second. 'As a matter of interest, did you ever manage to get to Ellie Landy's digs?'

He frowned. 'Of course I did – well, nearly, before I was diverted here by the control room.'

She took a deep breath. 'So you never actually spoke to the landlady who reported her missing?'

He hesitated. 'Er – no, not exactly.'

She stared at the roof of the car for a moment as if counting to ten. 'I just don't get you sometimes, I really don't.'

He looked down at his lap, a doleful expression on his face. 'Sorry, old girl,' he muttered, like a child admonished by a teacher. 'I know I'm a waste of space and I let you down – but thanks for covering for me anyway.'

She sighed her frustration, then slowly shook her head, unable to be angry with him anymore. It was always the same with Hayden. She doted on this gentle, overweight, untidy man of hers, with his public school accent and courteous old-fashioned ways, even though she sometimes felt like giving him a good hard kick into the twenty-first century which he inhabited with such obvious reluctance.

He was quite simply a throwback from a past era, someone who would have been more at home in a P.G. Wodehouse drawing room with Wooster and Jeeves. She had never known him to swear or lose his temper and his disorganized, easy-going approach to life could be absolutely infuriating for those who had to work with him. At the same time, however, he was the sort of thoroughly decent person whom it was almost impossible to dislike. And, though his rough, more streetwise CID colleagues certainly saw him as a real oddball, they tended to treat him and his eccentricities with a sort of patronizing tolerant amusement – which served to annoy her even more, especially as Ted Roscoe wasn't inclined to be so magnanimous towards him and Hayden seemed to delight in inadvertently dropping himself in it with the DI at every opportunity.

Why this big affable eccentric had chosen the police as a career, Kate just could not understand and yet, to be fair, he had been an asset to the team on more than one occasion, his laid-back style and untidy appearance belying a razor sharp mind and close attention to detail that had resulted in the successful conclusion of several high-profile cases. Maybe that was why he had survived for so long in the unforgiving detective environment.

'Just tuck your shirt in, will you?' she said finally and, throwing the door open, climbed out to meet the SOCO team as their white Scientific Investigations van bumped along the track towards them.

CHAPTER 2

ELLIE LANDY'S FORMER digs were in a red-brick end-of-terrace on the Bridgwater side of Highbridge and the sign in the window downstairs said 'Vacancies'. The middle-aged woman who opened the door had uncombed blonde hair and was wielding a cigarette in a tortoiseshell holder like a blackboard pointer. Her eyes lit up behind the matching tortoiseshell spectacles the moment she saw what she obviously thought were a couple of potential new paying guests on her doorstep. The glint soon faded, however, when Kate produced her warrant card and told her who they were.

'Not before time,' the woman snapped, stepping aside to let them into the hallway. 'I telephoned your lot hours ago.'

Kate threw Hayden a venomous look, but was all smiles when she faced the other woman again. 'And you are—?' she began.

'Daphne Snell. I own the place. And the little bitch I reported missing has done a bunk – in my opinion, to avoid paying what she owes me.'

Ah, Kate thought, so your phone call was not prompted by concern for your lodger's wellbeing then? What a surprise!

'When did she leave?' she asked.

'Three days ago after breakfast and she must have been in a hurry, 'cause she left all her stuff behind.'

'What sort of stuff?'

Snell shrugged. 'Clothes, personal things, you know.'

25

'Didn't that strike you as strange?'

'Why should it? She obviously couldn't be seen leaving with all her gear, could she? That would have given the game away.'

'How long was she here?'

'Only a couple of nights – arrived in some swanky new sports car. Haven't seen hide nor hair of her since.'

Kate was tempted to tell her that that could be because she had drowned but then thought better of it.

'But why wait three days before ringing us?'

Daphne Snell grunted. 'Been away at me sister's for the weekend. Son, Graham, has been looking after things here for me and he never thought to tell me until today.'

'Where is he now?'

'At the bookies probably. It's all he thinks about lately.'

'Did he actually see her drive away in her sports car?'

'Dunno, but the car's not out front now, so she must have driven off in it.'

'I don't suppose you can remember what sort of sports car it was?'

'MG, I think. Blue.'

Kate stared around the green painted walls of the hallway, picking up the distinctive smell of yesterday's cabbage on the stale air – probably coming from a kitchen at the end of the hall. Drawing back from the smoke from Snell's cigarette that was enveloping her like a fug, she said, 'Have you checked her room?'

Obviously the dragon had, but she wasn't about to admit it. ''Course not,' she said, lowering her gaze. 'I'm not one to do things like that.'

'But you said just now that she left all her things behind. How would you know that without checking her room?'

Snell scowled. 'What's this, the third degree?'

Kate smiled faintly, but didn't answer her. 'Mind if we take a look now?'

For reply, Snell simply shrugged again, took another drag

on her cigarette and said, 'Suit yourselves. I'll get you the spare key.'

Ellie Landy's room was on the first floor, just off the landing, a crooked figure 'three' on the door. At Kate's request, the dragon shuffled away in her tattered carpet slippers, leaving Hayden and herself to go through the room on their own – not that there was much to see.

The bed was neatly made up but, apart from some cosmetics, a paperback book and a clouded glass of water on the bedside cabinet, the only other immediate sign of occupancy was a large haversack on a chair in one corner. Both the single wardrobe and rickety looking chest of drawers turned out to be completely empty.

'She obviously wasn't intending to stay long,' Kate commented.

'Would you?' Hayden said with a short laugh, watching as she lifted the haversack off the chair and up-ended it on the bed.

It contained just a sponge bag and a meagre assortment of clothing, consisting of a pair of stout shoes, some skimpy lace knickers and bras, a couple of tops and a pair of corduroy trousers.

Hayden immediately seized on the underwear with a loud chortle.

'Get a load of this, old girl,' he commented, holding up a pair of black silk panties. 'Just the job, eh?'

Kate gave him an old-fashioned look as she checked out the haversack's side pockets. 'Wouldn't fit you, Hayd,' she said drily, 'so put them back, will you?'

He chuckled. 'You should get knickers like these,' he persisted, dropping them back on to the bed. 'Real turn-on, they are.'

Kate snorted. 'More of a turn-on than your bloody striped boxers anyway,' she retorted, then abruptly broke off, tugging something free of the pocket she was searching.

'And what's wrong with my boxers?' he exclaimed. 'I think they're pretty neat.'

'Mobile phone charger,' Kate snapped, ignoring his protestations and holding up a coil of black plastic wire with a plug on one end and a metal connector on the other.

Hayden made a face. 'So what?'

'It tells us she *did* have a phone with her.'

'Well, no prizes for guessing that. Who goes anywhere today without a mobile or tablet – especially a journalist.'

'But if the phone isn't here, she must have had it on her when she died?'

Hayden glanced up from the book, looking puzzled. 'I thought we'd already come to that conclusion, old girl, but, like the plod skipper said at the scene, she must have dropped it when she fell in the river. Simple enough explanation. Or maybe it just washed out of her pocket.'

Kate snorted. 'Funny that her wallet and ID card didn't wash out of her pocket at the same time – and another thing, where's her notebook if one wasn't found on her? I've never known a reporter to be without one. So, did she drop that too? Or was it washed out of her pocket, like her mobile?'

Hayden shrugged, ignoring the sarcasm and picking up the paperback book to leaf through it instead. 'Maybe uniform didn't look hard enough. Easy thing to miss, a sodden notebook, don't you think? And, after all, she was wearing an anorak which could have had several pockets, and the skipper admitted they hadn't carried out a thorough search, for obvious reasons.'

Kate nodded slowly and started returning the clothing to the haversack.

'Next stop, our coroner's officer then,' she said. 'He would have bagged up her clothes and personal effects after she was deposited at the morgue – and we need one of those business cards the skipper was talking about so we can contact her boss for details of next of kin.'

It was apparent that Hayden wasn't listening but staring at the paperback book with a heavy frown.

'Hayden?' Kate snapped, returning the haversack to the chair. 'Hello? Anyone in there?'

For a moment there was no response and then suddenly he turned towards her with the book open at the title page. 'What do you make of that then?' he queried.

Kate took the book from him and closed it to stare at the cover. *'The Way Through The Woods?'* she said, quoting the title. 'I didn't know you were an Inspector Morse fan?'

He shook his head impatiently. 'No, not that. Open it at the title page.'

With a bemused shrug, she did so. 'Signed edition?' she commented, closing it again. 'Lucky girl – or maybe not so lucky now.'

He sighed. 'Sometimes, Kate, you are so thick,' he said with uncharacteristic rudeness. 'Look at the facing page.'

She threw him a daggers look and re-opened the book to peer inside again, noticing the biro scrawl immediately now. 'Looks like "Fardmar 10.30",' she read aloud. 'What the hell does that mean?'

He shook his head. 'Look at it again. I think it says "Sandman 10.30", do you see it?'

Another shrug, 'OK, "Sandman". So what? Maybe she was into horse-racing. Could be the 10.30 at some race-track. Hardly relevant to us.'

He looked unconvinced. 'I might agree with you if she'd written San*down*. Sandown Park is quite a nice race-track in Surrey I've visited a couple of times but Sand*man?*' He shook his head. 'Never heard of that. And anyway, why would she write the name in a treasured novel, defacing the thing? And it's obvious that she wrote the note in a hurry, which is why you couldn't decipher it at first.'

Kate shook her head a couple of times. 'Hayden, we're investigating a drowning. What has a book with "Sandman

10.30" got to do with anything?'

He sighed, replacing the paperback on the bedside table. 'Don't know, old girl, but I've a feeling in my water that it's very relevant. Maybe it's an appointment – her mobile rang while she was reading and the book was the only thing she had to hand to write in.'

'OK, OK,' Kate said wearily. 'We'll look into it later – just to humour you – but right now, I'd like to have another word with the dragon downstairs to find out when her son is likely to be back from the bookies. It seems he was the last person to see Ellie Landy alive, so maybe he can throw a little more light on things.'

But, as it turned out, they had no need to speak to Daphne Snell, for Graham Snell opened the front door with his key and strode into the hallway just as they got to the foot of the stairs. There was no doubt who he was either – the resemblance to his awful mother was immediately obvious – and she herself clinched the fact anyway by shouting from the kitchen, 'Graham, the police are here,' even as Kate and Hayden stepped into view.

Daphne Snell treated them both to a sheepish grin. 'My son,' she explained unnecessarily and, apparently guessing that they would want to talk to him, waved a bony arm towards a door on the left. 'You can use the sitting room.'

Graham Snell appeared to be in his mid-twenties and he was certainly an oddball. Tall and thin, with brown curly hair and a wispy immature beard, he wore large tortoiseshell glasses, like those of his mother, and affected a permanent squint. Dressed in a stained blue fleece, green corduroy trousers and badly scuffed suede shoes which hadn't been laced up properly, he looked like a refugee from a backstreet soup kitchen and it was plain that he was very uneasy.

'Did you win?' Kate asked directly.

He frowned. 'Win?'

'At the bookies – your mum said you'd gone there.'

He forced a smile, but it only hovered briefly over the slightly crooked mouth and his gaze slid away from her as he plucked nervously at his fleece with the fingers of one hand. 'Lost thirty quid,' he said.

'Mug's game,' Hayden declared, looking him up and down critically.

Snell nodded, but said nothing more.

'Ellie Landy?' Kate went on. 'The lodger? I gather from your mother that you were here when she – er – left?'

He nodded again. 'Yeah, I'd just come back from the bookies. Saw her drive away in that blue MG of hers as I walked up the road.'

'Which way did she go?'

'Left, I think.'

'Any idea where she was heading?'

He shrugged. 'Not the faintest. Don't know much about her.'

'She didn't say "cheerio" then?'

'Never said a word. Just drove off.'

'Was she carrying anything – a bag or something like that?'

'Didn't notice. Guests come and go here all the time.'

'But when she didn't come back after three days, didn't you wonder where she had got to?'

'Yeah, I did. That's why I told my mother about seeing her leave.'

'So why wait three days to do that?'

'Didn't think about it until Mum asked me if I had seen her about lately and I realized she had done a runner.'

'Pretty girl, was she?'

He frowned. 'Didn't really notice.'

'Fancy her, did you?'

Even Hayden looked surprised by the question.

Snell looked confused and his face reddened. 'No,' he said defensively. 'Not – not my type.'

'Was she prettier than me?'

Now Hayden frowned, darting a swift warning glance in her direction.

Snell began to stutter and shake his head. 'N-no, I – I mean, yes – I don't notice things like that.'

To Hayden's obvious relief, Kate didn't pursue the subject anymore, but smiled at the confused young man. 'Thank you, Mr Snell. We'll be in touch if we need to speak to you again.'

Outside in the street, Hayden rounded on Kate. 'What on earth was all that about?' he snapped. 'You were out of order in there, old girl. You embarrassed the life out of that poor chap.'

Kate nodded, her eyes gleaming. 'That was the general idea, Hayd,' she said. 'I wanted to see his reaction to the suggestion that he might have had the hots for Ellie.'

Hayden raised his eyebrows. 'You think he may have done her in, is that what you're saying?'

Kate shrugged. 'If this job turns out to be more serious than an accidental drowning, he is likely to be a key suspect. He was the last one to see her alive and he's obviously seriously introverted – the sort of weirdo who nurses unsavoury urges—'

'Oh, poppycock!' Hayden snorted. 'He's just a shy youngster, that's all. I think you're getting paranoid in your old age.'

She sighed as they climbed back into the CID car. 'You're probably right there, Hayd, but at this stage in the game we have to consider all things. Talking of which, I think we should head back to the nick to see "Dr Death" and also get the plods out to look for any abandoned blue MG sports cars – that would at least give us an indication of where she went into the water.'

He grinned at her use of the coroner's officer's unfortunate nickname, then glanced at his watch. 'Lunch first, though, eh?' he suggested.

Kate shook her head again. "Fraid you're out of luck there, Hayd,' she said. 'Job first.' She prodded his stomach with one finger. 'You can afford to lose a bit of that flab anyway.'

CHAPTER 3

THE MAN AT the end of the telephone had a loose bubbling cough, and Kate visualized a fat little man hunched over an untidy paper-strewn desk in a dingy office, wreathed in smoke from the cigarette drooping from his mouth. Too much exposure to her father's collection of Philip Marlowe and Mike Hammer books as a child, she decided with a wry smile, waiting for the coughing to stop and for Gabriel Lessing of Lessing's Global News Agency to recover from the shock of what she had just told him.

A thorough examination of Ellie Landy's clothes in the presence of the coroner's officer had produced nothing of value – just two water-logged biros, a handkerchief and a packet of Polo mints. No mobile, notebook or car keys – not even a tape machine, but at least the business cards in the wallet had given her Gabriel Lessing, whatever that was going to be worth.

'Drowned, you say?' he wheezed into the phone.

'As far as we know, sir,' she replied. 'But there will have to be a post mortem to positively establish the cause of death.'

Another bout of coughing and an apology. 'Asthma,' Lessing explained in just above a whisper. 'I'll be OK in a minute – just the shock.'

For a moment Kate thought he had become overcome with emotion at the news of the tragedy, but he soon put her right there.

'What the hell am I going to do now?' he wailed. 'Them

floods is big news and she was right there – on the spot. We're only a small agency and with her dead, I'm bloody stuffed.'

'Nice of you to be so sympathetic,' Kate said with heavy sarcasm.

There was an angry snarl and more coughing. 'Don't give me that crap, love,' Lessing threw back, losing his calm for a moment. 'What do you want – a bleedin' eulogy?'

'It might tell us a bit about her anyway,' Kate responded drily. 'What can *you* tell us?'

'Not a lot,' he went on. 'Single. Used to live in Somerset – Glastonbury, she told me. Left and went to uni 'cause she didn't get on with her old man. Bit of a hot arse, I reckon – maybe that were the reason. Whole stream of boyfriends. I only took her on 'cause I was desperate – sort of work experience. But she were a good nose. Got some good stories for me—'

'How long was she with you?'

'About a year and a half. Then the flooding business come up and, as she knew the area, I thought I was on to a winner by sending her down there to cover it. Bloody shit out now, haven't I?'

Kate controlled her anger with an effort. 'Can you give me her home address?' she said. 'We'll need one of her parents to formally identify her.'

He grunted. 'Don't know whether you'll have much luck there, darlin'. I got the impression that they'd split up, so one or other of 'em might have already pissed off.'

Kate heard the rustle of paper and a few seconds later, he came up with the address. 'I might schlep down there meself, Sergeant,' he said after she had noted the details. 'Thinking about it, this could be a good story in itself. Where can I get hold of you?'

Kate put the phone down without any reply.

'Nice chap,' Hayden commented, having heard the conversation on the speaker.

Kate threw him a quick glance. 'I feel like a good wash after talking to that arsehole,' she replied and stood up. 'Anyway, I'd better pop over to Glastonbury and break the bad news to Ellie's dad.'

Hayden beamed. 'We could stop for a late lunch on the way back,' be suggested. 'I know a nice little place—'

'*You're* not going anywhere,' Kate reminded him and nodded towards the closed door of Roscoe's office. 'Your appraisal is in five minutes.'

His grin faded. 'Couldn't we tell the boss we had an urgent inquiry?' he pleaded. 'I mean, what's more important? My appraisal or this investigation?'

She smiled back, and pulled her coat off the back of the chair. 'Your appraisal, Hayd,' she replied, and headed for the door, jangling her car keys. 'Enjoy!'

The house was set back among trees on the outskirts of the town. A printed yellow Neighbourhood Watch sign on one wall announced, 'We do not buy or sell at the door', and someone had added in felt-tip pen underneath, 'So piss off!' It took Ellie Landy's father a long time to answer the bell and when he did, he stood there for a moment staring at Kate with a wild look in his dark eyes.

'What?' he said, his tone laced with aggression and his hands balled into bony fists.

He had to be in his early sixties, incredibly thin – almost consumptive – with straggly brown hair down to his shoulders and an unkempt beard streaked with grey.

'Mr Landy?' Kate queried and produced her warrant card. 'Detective Sergeant Kate Lewis, Highbridge police station.'

His eyes narrowed. 'Landy?' he echoed. 'What's that bitch said now?'

For a moment Kate was completely taken aback. 'I'm sorry, Mr Landy,' she said. 'Is there a problem?'

'Name's not Landy, it's de Marr,' he said, 'Lawrence de

Marr, as you well know.'

'And how should I know that, Mr de Marr?' she asked. 'I've never met you before.'

He snorted. 'Before your time, was I?' he sneered.

Kate was beginning to experience some bewilderment. 'So, Ellie Landy's not your daughter then?'

He laughed, not a pleasant sound. 'Oh, she's my daughter all right,' he said, 'or rather stepdaughter – but only because I inherited her.'

Kate took a deep breath. 'Look, Mr de Marr,' she said, 'I don't know what this is all about, but can I come in for a moment? I have some bad news.'

His eyes narrowed. 'Bad news? What sort of bad news?'

'I really think it would be better if I came in for a moment.'

He looked her up and down, his gaze strangely unsettling, and then he laughed again. 'Sure you want to?'

She didn't answer, but met his gaze with a hard one of her own. In the end, he shrugged and stepped to one side. 'Your choice,' he said. 'First door on the left.'

He followed her into what seemed to serve as a study-come-music room. The curtains were drawn, so much of the place was draped in gloom, but Kate could see a number of electric guitars displayed on the walls and an electronic organ under shelving crammed with books in one corner.

Indicating an armchair partially concealed by the open door, de Marr settled on to a swivel chair set in front of a large paper-strewn desk and waited for her to say something, a cynical smile hovering over his thin lips.

'Musician, are you?' she said, trying to ease into things and reduce some of the tension in the room.

'Used to be,' he said and laughed again. 'You really don't know who I am, do you?'

She shook her head. 'Perhaps you'd enlighten me.'

'Rod Tolan?' he said. 'At least, that was my stage name.'

She gaped, her subconscious throwing up the vision of a

leather clad man wielding an electric guitar and leaping across a spotlit stage in front of a weirdly dressed group to the screech of tortured acoustics.

'Well, I'm damned,' she breathed. 'The heavy metal band, Twisted Lizard. I bought your CDs as a teenager. You were top of the heap.'

'Yeah,' he grated, no sign of a smirk on his face this time. 'Well, I was once – but then that bitch, Landy, said I had been abusing her since she was fourteen.'

'I remember the case,' she said quietly, not really knowing what to say. 'I was in uni at the time.'

He jerked a packet of cigarettes out of his pocket, shook one into his palm and lit up, staring at the wall through the smoke as if unaware of her presence. 'I got four years. Wife left me, I went on the sex offenders register and my music career went down the toilet.'

His body jerked suddenly and his eyes re-focused on her face. 'Sorry you came in here now, Sergeant?' he said. 'I'm a dangerous man.'

For some reason, Kate didn't feel in the least bit threatened, merely uncomfortable. 'Did you do it?' she said.

He nodded. 'Yeah, 'course I did, but the little harlot asked for it. I just gave her what she wanted.'

'You really believe that?'

He shrugged. 'Who cares? It's done now anyway and I have to live with the consequences – as well as the hostility of everyone round here. Got a couple of bricks through my window last week. Didn't report it. What was the point? Your lot wouldn't have been interested anyway.' He turned in his seat to stub out his unfinished cigarette on the edge of the desk, then swung round to face her again. 'So, Sergeant Lewis, what's this bad news you've got for me? Don't tell me my ex-wife has been hit by a truck?'

Kate hesitated, not sure how he was going to take what she had to say under the circumstances. 'Not your wife, Mr de Marr,' she said. 'It's Ellie – I'm afraid she's dead. Her body was found in the River Parrett this morning and it appears that she drowned.'

'Ellie? Drowned?' For a second he just stared at her and then, to her horror, he threw back his head and laughed uproariously. 'Bloody hell, that's the best news I've heard in months, Sergeant; you're a star!'

Kate scrambled to her feet. 'I really don't think that's an appropriate thing to say, Mr de Marr, whatever you thought of her. For a young life to be so tragically lost in this way—'

'Bollocks!' he exclaimed. 'That bitch ruined my life and now she's got her just desserts. What do you expect me to do, cry?'

'No, Mr de Marr,' she said tightly. 'But we would like you to come to the mortuary to formally identify the body.'

He was on his feet too now, the wildness back in his eyes. 'Me? Identify Ellie's corpse?' and he laughed again. 'Sergeant, I would be delighted. Just say when.'

Kate bumped into Hayden the moment she walked into the CID office and he certainly didn't look his usual happy self. 'Good appraisal, Hayd?' she sniped with a grin.

He treated her to a sullen pout. 'The man is a cretin,' he muttered. 'Told me I was a lazy so-and-so who couldn't even get out of bed on time in the mornings.' He stared at her accusingly. 'You didn't tell him about today, did you?'

Kate grabbed his elbow and wheeled him out of the office into a small storeroom off the main corridor. 'No, I didn't tell him, Hayd,' she said. 'But everyone knows you are always late and you're not the most dynamic detective, are you?'

He snorted. 'I'm a thinker, you know that,' he huffed. 'It's the old cerebral thing with me.'

She grinned again and squeezed his arm. 'Maybe you should spend less time thinking and more time doing then, eh?' she suggested.

He manufactured a frown. 'That's very hurtful, you know, coming from one's own trouble and strife. It could give a chap a very serious inferiority complex.'

'Balls, Hayden!' she said pleasantly. 'You're not capable of having a complex.'

He beamed suddenly. 'You might be right there too, old girl,' he agreed with a wink, his natural humour suddenly breaking through the contrived resentment. 'So what about Ellie Landy's old man – did you manage to see him in the end?'

'Oh yes,' she said grimly, and told him of her shock discovery.

He whistled. 'A paedophile with a grudge, eh?' he murmured. 'Good job this isn't a murder. What with your suspicions about Graham Snell and now this character, Roscoe would be jumping out of his tree.' He hesitated and scratched his nose. 'Er, I've been thinking – you know that thing you said I shouldn't be doing any more – the note I found, "Sandman 10.30", could be the name of someone she had arranged to meet and it occurs to me that the Sandman in mythology is the chap who comes along and sprinkles magic sand in your eyes to make you sleep.'

'So? What are you saying? She couldn't sleep, so decided to call up the Sandman?'

He gave a genuine frown this time. 'Don't know really. Just strikes me as a bit odd. Could be a nickname or an alias, even the real name of someone. We should check the electoral role.'

'Which would get us where exactly, even if we found someone with that name?'

'We could ask the question?'

She snorted. 'Oh yes, that would be really clever – Sorry, Mr Sandman, but we found the same name in the front of a crime novel left behind by a drowned woman and wondered if you had ever arranged to meet her?'

He winced. 'Just thought it might be something we could

follow up on.'

She turned for the door. 'Try not to dwell on it, Hayd,' she said drily. 'We don't want you over-taxing that cerebral engine house of yours, do we?'

He waggled an admonishing finger at her. 'Lowest form of wit, sarcasm, you know, old girl. But sticking with it, is there the remotest chance that we might be going to eat sometime today, do you think?'

She sighed. 'There's cold ham in the fridge at home and chips in the freezer,' she said, turning back through the door into the corridor. 'I'll join you as soon as I've seen the boss.'

He rubbed his hands. 'Excellent. Give him my kind regards, won't you? And see if you can cheer him up.'

As it turned out, however, Roscoe was in no mood to be cheered up and his mood remained sour and uncommunicative throughout most of Kate's briefing on the progress of their inquiries. But his demeanour soon changed when she passed on her reservations about Graham Snell and Lawrence de Marr and he seized on the former rock star's name immediately.

'Lawrence de Marr?' he exclaimed, slapping the palm of one big hairy hand down on the table top. 'I *knew* I'd heard Ellie Landy's name somewhere. It was a Bristol case about five years ago. Didn't realize that dirty bastard, de Marr, had moved back down here when he came out of stir.' He extracted a wad of gum from somewhere under his moustache and dropped it with a dull thud into the wastepaper bin. Then, shaking a cigarette out of a packet on his desk, he tapped it several times on the desk top before lighting up and enveloping Kate in smoke.

'You know it's now illegal to smoke in the workplace?' she said tartly, waving some of the smoke away.

He ignored her and carried on with what he was saying.

'So, de Marr's back on our manor, is he? Well, that is food for thought. What with him and this Graham Snell weirdo you've just told me about, at least we've now got a couple of ready-made suspects to go for if this bloody drowning turns out to be something other than an accident.'

Kate stiffened in the straight-backed chair, her in-built antenna on full alert. 'Why do you say that, Guv? Something come up, has it?'

This time he waved the smoke away with a grunted apology, then stared at her for a moment. 'Don't go getting all excited,' he censured. 'As far as I'm concerned, we're still dealing with a straightforward drowning case. It's just that I've received a phone call from the coroner's officer to say that the PM, which was originally scheduled for Thursday, is now being brought forward to tomorrow and apparently the senior pathologist, Lydia Summers, is being called in to do it.'

Kate lurched forward in her chair. 'Tomorrow? Why on earth is that?'

He shrugged. 'Your guess is as good as mine, but apparently when they stripped her, they found something they're not happy with, so I want you there when they open her up. Ten o'clock sharp. Got it?'

Kate nodded. Great, she thought grimly. There was always something to look forward to as a police detective.

'Oh yeah,' Roscoe added, 'and take Sherlock with you – *if* he can get up in time!'

CHAPTER 4

THE SMELL WAS usually the first thing to hit the senses, but Kate and Hayden arrived at the mortuary in good time and well before the clinical butchery was due to take place. The naked body of the young woman was lying on her back on the stainless steel mortuary table, swollen by gas and the water from the River Parrett that would shortly be released by a razor sharp scalpel and Kate tried not to think about what she would have to witness when the macabre dissection got underway.

Despite being an experienced detective, who had seen more than her fair share of the macabre in her career, Kate had never got used to post mortems. It wasn't so much the gore and the smell, though that was bad enough, but the indifferent manner in which the cadaver of what had once been a living human being was treated by those charged with the duty of looking into the circumstances of their death. In life, the person had been a unique character; an individual, with his or her own likes, dislikes, opinions and aspirations, who had laughed, cried and loved. In death, however, they suddenly became an inanimate object, identified only by the label tied to their toe – a 'thing' to be stripped naked and stretched out on a steel table under the glare of powerful strip-lights, without any regard to privacy or decency, before being studied in minute humiliating detail and then callously dismembered with cold clinical precision.

It was a sobering thought that this was the fate that awaited so many people with the severing of their mortal coil and for Kate it was one inescapable truth that was the stuff of nightmares.

Yet the job had to be done. It was vital to establish the cause of a death when this was unclear from its initial incidence, otherwise it would be open to anyone to murder a relative or neighbour for revenge, personal gain or any of a number of motives that might prompt a homicide, without the slightest fear of detection. And the process had come a long way since the law to make post mortems mandatory in relevant cases had been passed in the nineteenth century. This had at first resulted in ham-fisted examinations being conducted in barns, sheds and even public houses by untrained, sometimes half-drunk physicians with little equipment and virtually no idea what they were supposed to be looking for. Resource-led sophistication was the order of the day in the twenty-first century, however, and every unnatural or violent death invariably resulted in a clinical investigation so thorough that absolutely nothing was left to chance.

Lydia Summers was already kitted out in her protective overalls and an assistant was standing by with the sophisticated video camera that would record the whole sickening process for the benefit of the coroner and the inevitable inquest, and the pathologist smiled as they walked into the room.

'So what have we got, Doc?' Kate said by way of introduction and also to take her mind off the more gruesome side of what was about to take place. 'We understood this was an accidental drowning?'

Summers nodded. 'Well, it was certainly a drowning, Sergeant, and I am sure that I will find the lungs marbled, spongy and swollen with fluid when I open her up. If you look at the nostrils and mouth, the traces of white froth you can still see exuding from the apertures is certainly characteristic of a drowning and undoubtedly this will also be present in the trachea and bronchi. But I'm not too sure about the rest of it.'

'Meaning what?'

Summers sighed, clearly enjoying the suspense she had created. 'You know, I always think pathology is very much like police detective work. Conan Doyle thought so too; that's why he created Sherlock Holmes after working with Dr Bell in Edinburgh. You can tell a lot from a corpse; build a complete picture as to what sort of person they were and how they died. It's all down to observation and conclusions based on the evidence that's presented before you—'

'OK, Dr Summers,' Kate interjected, making no effort to conceal her impatience. 'Elementary and all that but what have you got for us?'

'Ah,' the pathologist replied with an extravagant wink. 'Now that's the interesting part. Would you like to approach the bench, as I believe the judge says to lawyers at crown court?'

Kate was at the head of the corpse a fraction of a second before Hayden.

'See there,' Summers said, pointing with a gloved hand. Kate saw immediately what she was indicating – some greenish-brown marks at the lower end of the neck, just above the clavicles.

'Contusions,' the pathologist explained. 'Bruising essentially. The marks were noted by one of my attendants when the woman's clothes were removed.'

'Why weren't they spotted when the body was examined at the scene?'

Summers shrugged. 'Bruises have an individuality all of their own, Sergeant. The time element for bruises to become visible varies from person to person and can also be affected by the environment and ambient temperature.'

'So, what are your conclusions? That she was violently assaulted?'

Summers shook her head. 'Not in the way you mean. In my opinion, the marks may have been caused by a heavy relentless pressure, rather than by the kind of compression that occurs in a strangulation. In simple terms, it could be that her head was forced under the water and kept there until she asphyxiated.'

She nodded to a green-robed attendant, who seemed to be telepathic, for, without being told, he grasped the dead woman's right shoulder and bodily pulled her over on to her side, with her back towards Kate.

'See?' the pathologist continued.

Kate peered closer and drew in her breath sharply. The long, irregular green-brown marks were clearly visible across the shoulders, just below the nape of the neck.

'What do you think?' Summers queried, like a lecturer to a student at medical school.

Kate pursed her lips for a second, thinking, but it was Hayden who came up with the analysis. 'She was lying on something which pressed into her back?' he suggested. 'Something with an edge to it, like a piece of timber or a kerb?'

The pathologist gave him a thin smile. 'Very good, DC Lewis. But more likely a step or a river bank landing stage. There are contusions on her buttocks and the backs of her upper thighs too, suggesting contact with other raised surfaces, perhaps gravel or tree roots, plus bruising to her abdomen and hips, probably caused by a heavy weight pressing down on her body—'

'Maybe another person, is that what you're saying?' Hayden interjected again. 'Perhaps sitting astride her and pressing her against whatever it was she was lying on.'

An admiring glance from the pathologist this time. 'Bravo again, DC Lewis. The contusions would have been more pronounced had she been naked at the time, of course, but the thick anorak she was wearing cushioned the effects somewhat. And I think she may have struggled, as a result of which her assailant increased the pressure on her, in a determined effort to hold her down.'

Kate shuddered, horrific visions crowding her mind as she thought of what Ellie Landy must have gone through. 'So we're talking murder?' she said.

Summers shook her head. 'It's one hypothesis, Sergeant,' she said, 'but there are other possibilities and I could be completely wrong. It is not uncommon for corpses floating in a river to collide with debris, boat hulls, landing stages and so forth – hence the marks to her face and head, as dead bodies tend to float face-downwards – and, if you look at her left thigh, you will see the nasty tear, which looks as though it was made by barbed wire, possibly from a submerged fence. Another pathologist might consider that some of the specific marks I have drawn your attention to were also caused in this way. But you would have a job attributing the contusions on the neck and the marks on the back to this type of occurrence. I can only tell you what I see and what, in my professional opinion, could be a feasible scenario. As detectives, it is your job to try and put some meat on the bones, so to speak.'

As the attendant eased the body on to its back once more, Summers reached across to raise the dead woman's right arm and pull it towards her. 'There's one more thing,' she said. 'Look at the fingers of her right hand.'

Both Kate and Hayden did so and again Hayden was first in with a comment. 'Torn finger nails,' he breathed. 'A wall or something like it.'

Summers raised both eyebrows. 'You should be doing my job, DC Lewis,' she patronized. 'But you are certainly correct. Several of the nails are coming away from the fingers, which is normal in an immersion like this, but you can still see that

47

they have suffered substantial cuticle damage and there are traces of something beneath them, which I would suggest is a lot more than her own blood. I am convinced that she scraped her hand across a rough surface in the panic of imminent expiration – something rough and unyielding to cause those injuries – and a wall would be a good start.'

'Bloody hell,' Kate exclaimed. 'Roscoe's gonna love this!'

'I'll be arranging for toxicology and other specialist tests, of course,' Summers went on, 'so it might be a bit of a wait.' She smiled benignly. 'But the wait will be worth it, I'm sure. Now, if we're done, I have a post mortem to conduct.'

And she reached for the scalpel....

Kate was right about one thing – Roscoe was not happy with her news.

'Are you trying to say this could be a murder?' he snapped. 'Seem to be a lot of flippin' assumptions here.'

'A lot of unnatural bruising too, Guv,' Kate said. 'Best to play safe and treat it as suspicious, until we know otherwise.'

'All right for you to say,' the DI grumbled. 'But murder investigations cost a lot of ackers. Mr Ricketts, our ultra-cautious DCI, will need convincing before he's going to recommend a major crime inquiry. To be honest, we'd look bloody stupid if we set a hare running, only to find the silly bitch ended up in the river because she slipped on some dog shit.'

Kate winced. 'Your call, Guv,' she said. 'I can only relay Doc Summers' findings.'

He chewed furiously for a few moments, then stared her straight in the eye. 'So, what do *you* think?'

She shrugged. 'Lot of ifs and buts about this one, Guv,' Kate said. 'It's not like a straightforward strangulation or knifing where you've got definite evidence, but to my mind, several things don't add up.'

'Like what?'

'Like the missing mobile and notebook, for a start – and

her car ignition keys too. There was no sign of any of the stuff at her lodgings, although there was a mobile charger there, indicating she did have a phone, so how come they all fell out of her pocket, yet her ID card and wallet didn't?'

'She may not have had a notebook with her at all and she could have dropped the mobile when she fell in – just like the plod skipper suggested.'

'Oh come on, Guv, we've already covered that. A journalist without a notebook? It doesn't compute. And we searched her clothes thoroughly and all we found were a couple of biros. Why would she have biros and no notebook?'

Roscoe lit another cigarette. 'OK, I'll admit that at first sight it all seems a bit sus, but I'd need a lot more than we've got before I decided to recommend we sent the balloon up. So, as a start, when this arsehole, de Marr, turns up to do the ID in the morning, see what else you can find out from him about his daughter. And don't be going off at half-cock by treating him – or that fruitcake, Snell, for that matter – as a suspect in some fanciful murder investigation. OK? Also, get hold of that turd at the news agency again, see if he can shed any further light on things. Then report back to me PDQ with what you've got. Savvy?'

She nodded, then hesitated before coming out with what she had on her mind. He picked that up and raised an inquisitorial eyebrow. 'And?' he said. 'What else?'

She made a face. 'You won't like it.'

'Try me.'

'Hayden spotted something in her room.'

His eyes narrowed at mention of her husband's name. 'What's Sherlock come up with this time then?'

'It was a handwritten note in a paperback book on her bedside cabinet. It said "Sandman 10.30". Maybe she went to meet someone?'

His frown became a ferocious scowl. 'Sandman? Isn't that the fairytale dipstick who was supposed to send people to sleep by chucking sand in their eyes?'

'*Sprinkling* magic sand, Guv,' she corrected. 'But I wasn't thinking of fairytales. Could be a real person she was going to meet. That could be the connection we're looking for.'

'Yeah,' he agreed. 'And I can just see me going to the DCI to say we've got a possible murder and we think the key suspect is the bloody Sandman.'

She grinned, remembering an earlier conversation with him. 'A bit more convincing than the tooth fairy, though, Guv,' she commented. 'Wouldn't you agree?'

'Just sod off, Lewis!' he said. 'Before I forget I'm a bleedin' gentleman!'

CHAPTER 5

LAWRENCE DE MARR was dressed in what looked like his best suit when he turned up at the mortuary at eleven in the morning, following Kate's telephone call, but in a strange way his clothes made him look even more like a skeleton and the dark blue jacket looked at least two sizes too big on him.

'Thought I'd dress for the occasion,' he said with a grin and tossed his cigarette into the shrubbery beside the double doors. 'After all, it isn't every day you get to see your stepdaughter parked in a fridge, is it?'

Kate threw him a look of undisguised contempt as she led the way into the building, but his perverted humour was undiminished when one of the attendants showed him through to the viewing room and he emitted a throaty chuckle as he stared at Ellie Landy's waxen face.

''Strewth, girl,' he joked, 'you don't look at all well.'

'Is this your daughter or not?' Kate snapped, her eyes blazing.

He frowned. 'Stepdaughter,' he corrected. 'But yeah, that's her. I'd know that smug look anywhere. Been cut up yet, has she?'

He made to lift the corner of the sheet, which covered the body up to the shoulders, but Kate knocked his hand away and he grinned again.

'Just thought I'd take a look,' he said in mock protest. 'See if they stitched her up as well as she did me.'

51

'Perhaps you'd come through to the office,' Kate said coldly. 'There's a statement of identification we'd like you to sign.'

He shrugged and moved ahead of her in the direction of the doors she had indicated, lighting another cigarette in the reception area beyond and nodding to the coroner's officer as he brushed past him into a small side room.

'Do you know where Miss Landy's mother is now?' Kate queried as he signed the statement form and straightened up.

He nodded and this time there was no humour in his expression, just a bleak far-away look. 'Last I heard, she was in Rio,' he said, 'her and her new hunk. That was when I was in stir. Could be anywhere now.'

'So she has no other relatives?' Kate went on, disappointed that the formal identification had to rest with de Marr.

He studied her for a moment. 'No, love,' he said finally. 'Just good old jail-bird Lawrence. Is that a problem for you?'

She didn't answer him but went off on another tack. 'Was Ellie a fit sort of person?'

He drew heavily on his cigarette and blew smoke rings at the ceiling. 'Fit enough,' he said with another throaty chuckle. 'Did me the world of good at the time. Quite the athlete actually – won the triathlon at uni twice, I hear.'

Kate started. 'Triathlon? What did that involve?'

He made a face. 'Running, swimming, cycling – that sort of thing.'

'So she was a swimmer?'

'You'd have to be to a swimmer if you were swimming in a triathlon, wouldn't you, love?'

Kate's heart began to beat faster but he was ahead of her already and added, 'So how did she manage to drown, that's what you're thinking, isn't it?'

She made no reply again and his grin was back like a flash. 'You reckon someone did her in, don't you?' he said, his gaze locked on to her face. He leaned towards her and out of the corner of her eye, Kate saw the coroner's officer tense.

'Well, I'll tell you something for nothing, Detective Sergeant Lewis; you find the feller that did it and I'll buy him a drink!'

'Bloody hell,' Roscoe erupted after she had updated him on developments. 'You're determined to make this a murder job, aren't you?'

Kate shrugged. 'I'm just telling you what de Marr told me,' she said, 'and the fact that Ellie Landy was apparently a strong swimmer only serves to support the pathologist's view that she didn't just fall into the river and drown as a result of an accident. What we still don't know is precisely where she went in—'

'Which we're never likely to find out anyway unless we employ a flaming medium.'

Kate frowned at the interruption. 'That's not necessarily the case. There is Ellie's car. The blue MG I told you about earlier? I've already circulated a description of the motor and if the plods find it, it should significantly reduce our search area.'

Roscoe nodded, looking noticeably underwhelmed. 'Yeah, whatever. Thing is, I've seen the DCI and he's instructed me to treat the whole thing as a straightforward drowning, nothing more, unless we turn up something more substantial.' He made a grimace. 'Which means that for the time being I get to run the bloody inquiry, with just a basic team to do the business.'

'That could be a big mistake,' Kate observed. 'We need to hit this with everything we've got before the trail goes cold.'

He snorted. 'Tell me about it but, according to the boss, there is no trail yet. He's not convinced Landy's injuries are necessarily due to an assault. He suspects they could be the result of river damage, which he says he's seen several times before in his illustrious career. Also, because of the number of major incident inquiries currently running in the force, he reckons that resources are too stretched to justify the setting up of yet another one on the strength of what we've got so far.'

'He didn't know about the triathlon thing when you went to see him, though, did he?'

Roscoe cut her off with a wave of his hand. 'Don't even go there,' he growled. 'Decision's been made and we'll just have to get on with the job as best we can.'

'And how the hell do we do that without the proper resources?' she persisted. 'There are miles of flooded fields out there. Maybe we should enlist the help of Ratty from *The Wind In The Willows*!'

Roscoe's eyes hardened, but even as he made to snap back at her, his office telephone rang and, picking it up, he listened for a moment then replaced the receiver with a grim smile.

'Front office,' he said. 'Seems you have a visitor down-stairs – one Gabriel Lessing of Lessing's Global News Agency. Maybe you should start with him?'

Hayden opened the door of the interview room for Kate and followed her inside. Kate knew Gabriel Lessing immediately – even though she had never met him before. He was exactly as she had pictured him: short, overweight and balding, with thick slack lips, tiny restless eyes and thick squat fingers adorned with several large gold rings. Maybe her penchant for reading her father's collection of 1950s private eye novels had not been such a bad idea after all.

The little man affected an insipid smile as they entered the room, scrambling to his feet with one podgy hand out-stretched. Off his own turf, he seemed less sure of himself than he had been on the phone – altogether more subdued. 'Ah, you must be Detective Sergeant Lewis,' he said, the loose bubbling cough loitering at the back of his throat.

Kate's gaze took in the red bow tie, mauve shirt and shiny grey suit, noting the point of the red handkerchief visible above the line of the front pocket and smiled her distaste.

'My colleague, Detective Constable Hayden Lewis,' she said, nodding towards her other half.

Lessing raised both eyebrows. 'Same name, eh?' he commented.

'You usually do have the same name when you're married,' Kate said drily as she and Hayden dropped into two chairs facing the little man across the interview room table. 'Now, what can we do for you?'

Lessing followed their example and sat down again. 'Well, I – er – decided to come down here to see if I could help your inquiries in any way,' he replied.

Kate smirked again, reading him like a book. You mean, what's the story and is there anything in it for me? she mused. 'You could tell us a bit about Ellie Landy,' she encouraged.

'So it *is* her then?' he queried. 'She *has* been positively identified?'

'By her stepfather,' Kate replied.

'Oh? Stepfather? I didn't realize he wasn't her real old man. Who – who is he?'

Kate shook her head. 'I'm sorry, I can't tell you that. He might not want his name divulged.'

Lessing visibly started. 'Oh, why is that? Is he some sort of public figure?'

'I can't tell you that either,' she replied, knowing that the first thing he would do when he left the police station would be to find out and when he did, the 'whatnot' would really hit the fan in publicity terms.

The journalist looked irritated by her reply, but he didn't pursue the matter any further, instead launching into another question. 'Whereabouts was she found?'

Hayden sighed heavily. 'I thought you had come down here to help us with our inquiries, Mr Lessing?' he said.

The agency man nodded quickly. 'Of course – I'm just curious as to how this could have happened. She was a strong swimmer, you know.'

Kate nodded. 'So we understand. But you said on the phone that she was covering the flooding problem on the Levels? What was her angle?'

'Angle?' Lessing seemed indignant at her use of the term. 'My agency doesn't have angles, Sergeant. We just report the facts.'

'OK, so what "facts" was she specifically looking at?'

Lessing smirked, acknowledging that she was asking him exactly the same thing, but couched in a different way. 'The flooding should never have happened, we all know that, and her job was to look beneath the surface and see if there was any reason why the flood defences had not been upgraded.'

'So, dig up the dirt wherever she could?'

He hesitated, then sighed. 'Look, I have a business to run and that business depends on—'

'Scandal,' Hayden cut in.

Lessing shrugged, unperturbed by the accusation. 'If you like, yes. Good news doesn't sell newspapers.'

He leaned forward across the table, his eyes gleaming with excitement.

'You don't think her death was accidental, do you, Sergeant? You think someone did her in? Have they done a PM? What was the result?'

Kate ignored the questions. 'Do you know what she had found out?' she asked quickly. 'Anyone she was due to interview?'

Lessing shook his head. 'But she did ring me about two days ago to say she had stumbled on something unconnected with the flooding,' he said, 'which could be a major story.'

'What sort of thing?'

'I haven't the faintest. But it sounded big – that's why I was so gutted when you rang me to say what had happened.'

'And there was me thinking you were upset by her tragic death,' Kate said sarcastically.

Lessing gaped. 'Well, I was that as well but—'

'Did she say she was going to meet someone?' Hayden cut in.

The little man shook his head. 'Only that it would push the flooding to the inside pages.' He hesitated. 'She did mention a name, but it didn't make any sense to me.'

'A name?'

'Yeah, Sand something or other. Didn't quite catch it on the phone – bad signal with her mobile.'

Kate glanced quickly at Hayden but just in time stopped herself from blurting out the name that was forming on her lips. 'Sand, you say?'

'Yeah, Sandley, Sanders, something like that. Then we got cut off.'

'When was this?'

'Friday last, I think. She never rang again.'

No, Kate thought, because by then she was dead! 'I gather she had a blue MG sports car?' she went on, abruptly changing tack.

He was taken aback for a moment. 'Er – yeah, bought it at the end of last year. Why are you asking about the car?'

Kate shrugged. 'If we can find it, it might help us to determine where she went into the water. Do you know the registration number?'

He shook his head. 'No idea,' he replied dismissively, then leaned forward towards her, his eyes gleaming – obviously sensing a possible 'in' with the inquiry. 'Listen, Sergeant,' he said quickly, 'we could help each other, you know. Sort of pool information, if you'll pardon the pun. You can trust me not to release what you tell me until you give me the go-ahead. And I could be very useful to you out on the ground. Digging up information is my stock in trade.'

Kate stood up abruptly. 'I'll bear that in mind, Mr Lessing,' she said, 'but for the present there really isn't anything I can tell you. Best if you went back to London. Nothing you can do here.'

Lessing also stood up but stared her out. 'I'll be staying on for a while,' he replied defiantly. 'I'll probably see you around.'

Not if I can help it, Kate thought, but smiled and said, 'Thank you for your help, Mr Lessing,' and she nodded at Hayden to show him out.

Kate didn't make any move to leave the interview room but settled her bottom on the corner of the table and waited with her arms folded across her chest. Just minutes later Hayden practically bounded back into the interview room, as she'd known he would, his eyes alight with excitement. 'See, old girl? What did I tell you?' he exclaimed. 'Sandman! That note in the book *did* mean something.'

She nodded. 'Bravo, Hayd, but what?'

'Well, as I thought, Ellie Landy had obviously arranged to meet this feller somewhere.'

'Or woman,' she replied. 'Why should it have been a man necessarily?'

'Let's leave the pedantry out of it,' he retorted irritably. 'The important thing is that we now have a name—'

She smiled faintly. 'Which, according to you, belongs in a fairytale.'

He ran the fingers of one hand through his mop of untidy hair and began pacing the room. 'So what do we do now?' he said. 'We seem to have hit a brick wall.'

She shook her head. 'Not entirely,' she corrected. 'There is one avenue we could try first.'

'Which is?'

'Her mobile.'

'But there's no sign of it. It's probably at the bottom of the Parrett.'

'So, let's ring it,' she said, waving one of Ellie Landy's business cards in front of his nose. 'You never know, someone might answer it.'

So they did and it was with a sense of shock that they

heard the answer phone respond, 'You've reached the mobile of Ellie Landy. Sorry I'm not available just now. Please leave a message and I'll get back to you.' It was the soft husky voice of a dead woman, which filled the room with a ghostly presence that chilled right through to the bone.

'Want to leave a message?' Hayden asked with a twisted grin. 'Maybe some entity from the spirit world will come back to us with a reply.'

Kate studied him for a moment. 'Not funny, Hayden,' she said, 'not funny at all.'

CHAPTER 6

HE STOOD IN the curtained room with his back to the roaring log fire, watching the inky shadows climb the walls in front of him, the mobile phone in his hand and a thoughtful look on his face.

So, someone had called, had they? But no message had been left and the caller's number had been withheld. It had been a good idea to keep hold of the interfering bitch's phone. After all, he had no idea whom she might have spoken to before he'd got to her, but discovering a missed call to her number made several days after her death was unsettling. It could have been just a friend, catching up on any news, or a worried parent or boyfriend, wondering why she had not been in contact for a while. But on the other hand, it could have been someone she had confided in about the things she had discovered and if that were the case, he might soon have a serious problem on his hands.

Crossing the room to the drinks cabinet in the corner, he poured himself a single malt, holding the spirit in his mouth for several seconds as he pondered the issue. He had heard on the local television news that the woman's body had been found, but from the details released it seemed that the death was being treated as a tragic accidental drowning. The fact that the police had not come knocking on his door suggested that no one had alleged anything different, which meant that the person who had made the call to the mobile was either unaware of the circumstances or was intending to use information they had been given for personal gain.

He smiled grimly. If the former, there was nothing to fear and if the latter, then he would wait for the approach that would inevitably be made and take the action required to remove any threat that might present itself. And he allowed the whisky in his mouth to slip slowly down his throat before draining his glass.

Kate was filling her chipped mug from the coffee machine in the CID office when the telephone on her desk bleated urgently. Sipping from her mug, she returned to her desk and lifted the receiver. The control-room operator was brief. 'DS Lewis? Call for CID, skip.' Seconds later a sharp click preceded the rasp of someone breathing heavily.

'Detective Sergeant Lewis,' Kate said. 'Can I help you?'

'The drowning of that reporter,' a woman's voice blurted after a few moments' strained silence. 'I want to speak to the officer in the case.'

Kate set her coffee mug down on the desk with a frown. 'Who is this?' she queried.

'Never mind that,' the caller replied. 'Is it you or not?'

Kate beckoned to Hayden as he entered the office and switched the telephone on to speaker. 'I am one of the investigating officers, yes,' she said. 'What can I do for you?'

There was further hesitation before the woman answered. 'It wasn't an accident,' she said eventually.

Kate threw a swift glance at Hayden who was leaning over her shoulder, now with his head on one side as he listened intently. 'What makes you say that?' she went on.

'She was on to things,' the woman said.

Kate felt her heart start to race. 'What things?'

'*He* couldn't allow that.'

'Who is "he"?'

A harsh unamused chuckle. 'Your worst nightmare.'

Kate sighed, irritated by the clichéd phrase and suspecting she was dealing with a hoax call. 'Listen, love,' she said heavily, 'I am not here to play silly games with you. Exactly who are you and what have you got to tell me?'

Hayden tutted at Kate's impatience and squeezed her arm in warning, but he was too late. 'Sod you then,' the woman retorted and hung up.

'Well, that was nicely done, old girl,' Hayden commented drily. 'You really handled that like a pro.'

Kate glared at him. 'I can do without your sarcasm, thank you,' she snapped. 'It was obviously a rubbish call.'

He shrugged. 'Then how did she know the dead woman was a reporter? As far as I know, that info hasn't been released to the press yet.'

Kate snorted. 'OK, clever clogs, so make yourself useful and see if you can get the caller's number traced.'

'Is that before or after lunch?'

'What do *you* think?'

He stood to attention with a mocking grin. 'Right away, Sergeant.' And, turning sharply on his heel, he marched out of the room like a soldier on parade.

Kate glanced over her shoulder at his retreating figure and shook her head wearily. Sometimes Hayden could be such a child. But, though she hated to admit it, she knew his criticisms had been more than justified; she had been far too impatient with the woman caller and consequently might have lost a valuable witness. 'Damn, damn, damn!' she muttered to herself.

Retrieving her coffee mug, she took another sip, then pushed it to one side with a grimace. It was only lukewarm. So what now? Hope that the woman's number could be traced or simply wait in the hope that she would ring again? Somehow she felt that the latter option was pretty unlikely, but she was wrong. In fact, it was just ten minutes later that her desk phone rang and control put the same caller through.

'DS Lewis?' the familiar voice queried and before she could reply, the caller added, 'Meet me.'

Kate froze in her seat. 'Where?'

'Do you know the old derelict Toliver factory on the out-skirts of Street?'

Again Kate was given no opportunity to respond one way or the other, for the next instant, the caller snapped, 'One-thirty. Be there or you'll never hear from me again – and just you, none of your buddies.'

Then the phone went dead.

Kate glanced at her watch. 12.55. She looked around the office. The place was deserted – even Roscoe was not at his desk behind the glass partition that served as his private space – and, if she knew Hayden, he would be down in the canteen, stuffing his face before following up the inquiry she had given him. No time to arrange backup; there would be too many questions to answer first. She knew the risks, but she had no choice save to go it alone or chance making yet another faux pas which could lose her the mysterious witness altogether. Grabbing her coat and her all-singing, all-dancing TETRA police radio, she headed for the door.

Street was not a very picturesque village and it had never been one of Kate's favourite places – except for the huge commercial outlet site, with its wall to wall shopping oppor-tunities. But the Toliver factory was some distance from the village centre, accessed by a nondescript tarmac cul-de-sac, boasting a prize collection of potholes.

Toliver's was one of several similar abandoned properties and the previous owners of the one-time packaging company had not even bothered to secure the rusted metal gates with a padlock before they had left the building to rot.

Kate arrived in fragile sunlight a couple of minutes before the appointed time and, parking up on some waste-ground just before the entrance, she squeezed between the partially open gates into a large rubbish-strewn yard beyond.

The broken windows of the factory seemed to gape at her in surprise as she made her away across the yard to the yawning gash at one end of the building, which looked as though it had once been a loading bay, and a mangy tortoise-shell cat paused in the process of inspecting a clump of tall weeds erupting from the concrete apron to give her a wary once-over before streaking ahead of her into the opening.

She had remembered to bring a torch with her from the car, but there turned out to be just enough light penetrating the loading bay to enable her to see where she was going and she made her way among a litter of broken packing cases to some double doors at the far end. The doors opened with a protesting groan and she was presented with shards of light tracing a pattern of square window frames across a vast concrete floor from skylights thirty feet or so above her head.

'Hello?' she called a little self-consciously. 'Anyone here?'

A low wind breathed temporary life into the building, rattling window frames and stirring timbers, but that was the only response she received, for otherwise, the place appeared to be completely dead.

The tortoiseshell cat put in another brief appearance, emerging from behind some rusted wheeled bins a few yards away to stand there staring at her again for a few moments then it too was gone, strutting away back into the shadows behind the bins.

Turning around a full circle, she checked as much of the building's interior as she could make out in the grey gloom, using her torch to probe areas cloaked in shadow, but there was no sign of anyone and, clearing her throat and feeling more than a little silly, she called out again, 'Anyone here? If you don't show yourself, I'm leaving.'

But there was still no response – not even a single 'mew' from the cat, which appeared to have gone into hiding for good – and she frowned. Maybe the call had been a hoax after all and she was simply talking to herself. 'You've been had, my girl,' she murmured ruefully, and turned back towards the doors leading out to the loading bay. 'Time to go.'

She heard the loud bang almost at the same moment and swung in the direction of the sound. She hadn't noticed the side door some twenty feet away and the young woman had entered the factory through it, apparently deliberately slamming it behind her to attract her attention.

Kate walked slowly over to her, stopping some two to three yards short, when the other woman tensed and held up both hands in an arresting gesture, warning, 'No closer or I'm out of here.'

Kate studied her curiously. Even in the gloom she could see that she was no more than nineteen or twenty, with purple-streaked, shoulder-length blonde hair and a couple of brass rings through her lower lip and one in a nostril. She was wearing threadbare blue jeans, Doc Martin style boots and a heavy fawn–coloured fleece. Almost certainly a dosser, maybe also a user.

'Were you the person who rang me?' Kate queried.

The woman snorted. 'No, it was me twin sister – what do you think?'

Kate smiled faintly. The familiar sneering bravado, the usual attempt to appear hard and cynical. She had seen it all so many times before. Outwardly tough and confident, but inside nervous and vulnerable. This was damaged goods, but hopefully, not too badly damaged to be of value.

'What's your name?'

The other shook her head. 'No names.'

'So what shall I call you?'

'OK, Polly – you can call me Polly.'

'Is that your real name?'

'It'll do.'

'So, Polly what?'

'Polygon – the bleedin' dead parrot – I said no names.'

'And what have you got to tell me?'

'Depends what it's worth.'

Kate sighed. 'Look, love, I'm not here to play games with you. I told you that before. If you've got some information for me, let's have it and then we'll talk about how much it's worth.'

A harsh humourless laugh and the young woman lit a cigarette, choking for a moment on the smoke. Kate noticed that the hand holding the cigarette was shaking. Drugs? Probably coke or Big H, she thought. 'Think I'm stupid, love? A ton is what I want for this.'

It was Kate's turn to snort her derision. 'You have to be joking. We don't pay that sort of money.'

'Fifty then.'

'Give me something good and I can let you have a pony right now.'

'Twenty-five quid? You're having a laugh.'

Kate shrugged, hoping her bluff would work. 'OK, then I keep my money and you forfeit your next fix.'

Silence for a moment, then the woman dropped her cigarette and trod on it. 'If *he* finds me, I'm dead, and it'll be all down to you.'

Kate was unmoved. 'If *who* finds you?'

'Bread first.' A gloved hand shot out almost with the speed of a lizard's tongue.

Kate shook her head. 'No way. You'll just have to trust me.'

A brief pause and then the woman blurted, 'They call him the Sandman.'

For some unaccountable reason, Kate felt a chill run down her spine. 'Why Sandman?' she said, trying to keep the excitement out of her voice.

A further harsh laugh, but again there was no humour in it. ''Cause he puts people to sleep, that's why – just like in the kids' story. You savvy?'

'Did he put the reporter to sleep?'

There was a muffled curse. 'I told her to watch out for herself, but the stupid cow wouldn't listen. She must've got too close.'

'So you're saying the Sandman stiffed her?'

The sneer was back on the woman's face. 'No, I'm saying they went for a romantic dip together – are you stupid or what?'

Kate resisted the urge to slap her across the face and tried instead to count to ten, getting as far as five. 'So, who is he, this Sandman?'

'Dunno. No one knows. But he seems to have loads of stuff – whatever anyone wants, if they got enough bread.'

Kate's eyes narrowed. 'What sort of stuff?'

Another shrug. 'PCP, crack, you name it.'

'How do you know about him?'

'How'd you think I know? I ain't shivering 'cause I'm cold. I gets my stuff from one of his pushers. The guy's real flash and he's got a big mouth.'

'Who's the guy?'

Polly hesitated, then shrugged with a sort of desperate resignation. 'Leroy – Leroy Joseph. We've all been getting our stuff through him.'

'So why turn grass and bite the hand that feeds?'

''Cause the hand won't feed no more, that's why. I blabbed to that bleedin' reporter, when she come snoopin' around, didn't I? She must've said what I told her before she copped it, 'cause word on the street is that Leroy is out looking for me. I got to split before he finds me, maybe disappear to the Smoke, but I need some bread for the road.'

'For your next fix, you mean?'

'For the next few fixes, more like. I know another guy where I can get some stuff but I got to move fast.'

There was a loud 'crack' from somewhere else in the building and Polly noticeably stiffened, glancing quickly towards the loading bay area. 'I got to go. Give me the bread now.'

Kate thought about Roscoe as she produced her wallet and counted out twenty-five pounds in notes, wondering whether the crusty old sod would be prepared to grant the necessary retrospective authority for payment out of the CID informants' fund to enable her to claim the money back.

'You need to tell me a lot more than you've told me so far before I can give you anything,' she said. 'But I have it here if you want it.'

There was an angry snarl and the woman stepped forward a couple of paces, her fists clenched. 'You slag, I've told you too much already.'

Kate stood her ground. 'How will I find this Sandman?' she persisted.

Polly abruptly sagged back against the door through which she had entered the place. 'Maybe he'll find you first,' she grated, clutching at her stomach with both hands. 'Look, I need that fix. *Please....*'

Kate counted out a further twenty-five. 'Fifty if you give me what I need.'

The woman's gaze fastened on the money in her hand with a greedy intensity. 'Ask for Leroy at the Sapphire Club,' she blurted. 'They call him "the Spliff".'

Kate smiled grimly, knowing only too well that a spliff was a cannabis joint. 'Appropriate,' she commented.

Polly nodded quickly. 'He does most of the legwork for the Sandman,' she finished. 'But I reckon he's been dealing on the side and the Sandman won't like that one little bit if he finds out.'

Another loud crack from somewhere close by and Polly came off the door in a rush, one hand still clutching at her stomach, but with her gaze now riveted on the loading bay doors.

'I got to get out of here,' she whispered. 'I could've been followed. Sandman has eyes everywhere.'

Before Kate realized what she was intending to do, the

terrified woman suddenly lunged forward and snatched the money from her hand. Then, wrenching open the door behind her, she was gone, her footsteps ringing away on a concrete floor as she disappeared into what turned out to be a labyrinth of corridors and offices on the other side.

'Damn, damn, damn!' Kate snarled for the second time that day.

DI Roscoe was in a foul mood. 'So let me get this straight,' he rasped, staring Kate straight in the eye. 'You fixed up a meet with some bleedin' hophead without telling a soul about it, parted with fifty quid in exchange for some bullshit fairytale and then, to cap it all, let the conniving little bitch have it away on her toes?' He stabbed a finger forcefully in her direction, his head thrust forward aggressively. 'And now – and now you expect me to pay you the money back out of the informants' fund? Is that about right – have I covered everything?'

His voice couldn't have been any louder and, despite the fact that the confrontation was taking place in his office behind a closed door, Kate was quite sure that Hayden and her other colleagues sitting in the main CID office were able to hear every word and her toes almost curled up in embarrassment.

'Sorry, Guv,' she said limply. 'But I had no time to tell anyone where I was going and I am convinced Polly was telling me the truth.'

He snorted. 'Oh, Polly, is it? You're even on first-name terms, are you? Did she by any chance give you her telephone number and bust measurement as well?'

Kate winced, but thought it best not to say anything in reply.

'Polly!' Roscoe snarled derisively and shook his head in disgust. 'You've done this before on other jobs, if I remember rightly, haven't you, Miss? Gone off on your own like the flamin' Lone Ranger? You never learn, do you? Have you any idea what could have happened to you in that factory? It might have been a junkies' shooting gallery, full of dirty needles and lid-off crazies and you just walked in there like soddin' Alice In Wonderland!'

'Sorry, Guv,' she said again, then added, 'I suppose my fifty quid is down the drain now, is it?'

For a moment Kate thought Roscoe's eyes were going to erupt from their sockets, but he controlled himself with an effort. 'Get out of my sight, *Sergeant*,' he breathed and nodded towards the main office. 'And take that dipstick of a husband with you. We'll talk again tomorrow morning – by which time I might have cooled down.'

'By the sound of it, that was another job well done, old girl,' Hayden murmured to her as they quit the building.

'Shut it!' Kate retorted savagely. 'Or you can get your own bloody dinner!'

CHAPTER 7

THE SAPPHIRE NIGHT CLUB was well known in police circles. Its much publicized events, referred to as 'club nights', were a popular haunt of dispossessed youngsters, from as far afield as Bristol and Exeter, looking for a hedonistic night out, fuelled by illegal drugs and cheap alcohol; the place had been raided twice in the first six months of its opening. More recently, however, under new management, it had ostensibly smartened itself up, presenting a more acceptable image and earning itself some respite from the attentions of the police and local authority who had seemed willing to adopt a more flexible policy of co-existence with their noisy decadent 'tenant' in a new spirit of tolerance.

Kate hadn't told Roscoe that Leroy 'the Spliff' operated from the Sapphire Club. Somehow she hadn't felt that he would have been too receptive to the plan she had devised and she had decided, despite the obvious risk to her career, to go ahead with it, minus his blessing.

Hayden could have been a big stumbling block, for there was no way he would have agreed to what she was contemplating, but then fate had intervened; poor old Hayden had been called out from dinner to attend a complaint of assault occasioning actual bodily harm, leaving her free to pursue her plan with impunity.

She smiled as she parked her Mazda MX5 in the shadows of the night club's car park at just after eight in the evening, wondering what her colleagues would have said to see her striding towards the front doors in her very brief sequinned top and black trousers, with the cold night air brushing her bare midriff and her auburn hair brushed out over her shoulders.

The burly bouncer treated her to a lascivious grin as she flounced past him, her silver coloured shoulder bag bouncing on her hip, and, despite the club rule of 'no singles', he made no attempt to stop her, his gaze focused instead on her pierced navel as a second man sitting at a strategically placed table just inside the door accepted her twenty-five pounds entrance fee with an extravagant wink and issued her with a ticket.

The music – if it could be termed that – had greeted Kate from the car park itself, but in the foyer of the building she was conscious of the very floor beneath her feet trembling to the cacophonous challenge erupting from the other side of the pair of heavy wooden doors at the far end of the room and when she hauled open the right-hand door, brushing past another thug-like doorman on the other side, she stepped into a mayhem of mind-blasting rock music and writhing bodies, illuminated by brilliant flashing lights that threatened to turn her eyes inside-out.

For a few moments she stood by the wall, studying the faces constantly emerging, disappearing then re-emerging in the surrealistic glare of the flashing spotlights, trying to gauge the average age of the shaking, twisting, whirling figures. It had been her one concern that – at thirty – she might stand out like a sore thumb in a predominantly teens and early twenties crowd. But she was relieved to see several more mature men and women on the floor – some of whom looked even older than she was, and, relaxing a little now, she skirted the dancers and approached the red leather-clad bar with a smile and her purse in her hand.

There seemed to be an army of bar staff, men and women, flitting like wraiths among the on-off shadows, dispensing a

SANDMAN

variety of drinks to the crush of customers, many of whom she suspected were well under age. But in addition to stamina, the male bar staff also seemed to have excellent eyesight, and she was spotted almost immediately by a tubby thirty-something barman with oily black hair and a strong Southern Irish accent.

'Sure, an angel's just walked into my life,' he charmed, his voice raised to enable him to compete with the noise. 'What'll ye have, me darlin'?'

Kate smiled back. 'Any red wine?' she mouthed, leaning across the bar towards him, and in the next spotlight flash, she saw him start back from the bar in feigned shock. 'Red wine?' he echoed. 'Holy Mother, 'tis a terrible thing for a wee angel, like yourself, to be askin' a true Irishman for red wine.'

He produced a bottle of Bushmills whiskey and poured her a stiff measure. 'There y'are, me darlin'. A dram to be proud of. This one's on the house too, so it is.'

It was not the time or the place to argue the point and she nodded her thanks, picked up the glass and took a sip. He grinned at her, ignoring the sharp critical comments of his overworked colleagues, who plainly felt he should be getting on with the job instead of chatting up a pretty customer, and nodded towards the far end of the bar, inviting her to join him there.

'Sure, you must be from the old country with hair like that?' he shouted again, and this time he leaned across the bar towards her, stripping her clothes off with his eyes.

She shook her head, taking another sip of her drink to play for time as her mind raced. This could be a very profitable accident. If he was one of the regular barmen, he should know Leroy, the Spliff and that could short circuit a lot of otherwise dodgy inquiries.

'No, English through and through,' she shouted back, giving him another encouraging smile.

He affected an idiotic gaping expression – a proper

comedian, this one, she mused grimly. 'English?' he exclaimed. ''Tis a real tragedy, that is. An' there's me thinkin' what a quare cracker this wee Irish colleen is.'

His fingers brushed the back of her hand as she held her glass loosely on the bar top and instinctively her own hand clenched. He didn't seem to notice, but unwittingly provided her with the opportunity to ask the question that was burning on her lips, when he said, 'Sure, a pretty girl like yourself hasn't come here all on her own, has she now?'

She affected a shrug and deliberately glanced behind her into the blaze of spotlights. 'I wondered if Leroy was here tonight?' she said.

'Leroy?' he echoed and it was plain he hadn't the faintest idea who she was talking about.

She took a chance, forcing a laugh. 'Yes, they call him the Spliff. I was hoping he might have something for me.'

Again his expression was blank. 'Canna help ye there, darlin',' he said. 'But I'm here an' that could be a quare blessin' for a lonely lass like you.'

His hand reached across the bar and closed on her wrist. 'Why don't you an' me take a wee dander outside, eh?'

Unable to help herself, despite the circumstances, she tore her wrist free, pitching her glass of whiskey over his hand. 'Please, no!' she exclaimed.

His eyes immediately narrowed and his mouth twisted into a vicious scowl. 'Please, no?' he threw back at her. 'Please, no? Y'wee bitch—'

The tall thin man who had suddenly appeared at her elbow interjected with a sharp rebuke. 'Are you serving here?' he shouted. 'I want a double whisky. Famous Grouse.'

The barman glared at him but, under sideways glances from his nearby colleagues, he reluctantly capitulated. Grabbing a glass from under the counter, he turned towards the optics behind him.

'And another drink for my girl too,' the new arrival

shouted, nudging her with his elbow.

Furnished with the two whiskies, the stranger tossed a twenty pound note on to the counter and turned his back on the barman, leading Kate gently away from the bar to a corner of the room.

Kate raised her glass to her deliverer. 'Thank you – er—?' she began, shouting close to his ear.

'They call me Horse, love,' he said, raising his glass to hers and shaking his mane of black shoulder-length hair out of his eyes. 'And you obviously like to live dangerously. That guy had his sights set on you big time.'

She frowned, studying his thin bearded face and sharp dark eyes in the sudden blaze of a spotlight. 'Why do they call you Horse?' she queried with a smile.

He grinned, exposing even white teeth. 'A lady shouldn't ask that,' he retorted. 'It's all down to assets.'

She started, relieved that the gloom hid her embarrassment. 'Oh,' she said with a wry grimace. 'Sorry.'

He laughed. 'Don't be. I'm not.' He seemed to hesitate. 'But I couldn't help overhearing what you said to that Irish git at the bar. How do you know the Spliff?'

'Er – I don't.'

'Then why do you want to see him?'

'Without being rude, that's my business.'

'Looking for a fix, are you?'

She took a chance. 'Maybe I am.'

He thought for a moment, sipping his drink and leaning over her with one hand supporting him against the wall behind her. 'What are you on?'

She thought quickly and blurted, 'Coke.'

He finished his drink and straightened up, setting down his glass on a convenient table. 'Outside,' he shouted, nodding towards the entrance doors. 'We need to talk. Can't do it in here.'

She hesitated. She didn't know him from Adam and, once

outside the club, she could be at serious risk. On the other hand, though, why was she here? To find Leroy, of course. And this long-haired stranger seemed to be her only chance of doing that.

Draining her own whisky, she dumped her glass beside his and followed him out through the doors, the bouncer and his companion grinning knowingly when they saw the two of them leaving together. 'Have fun,' the bouncer said with a chortle which died abruptly when Kate's escort threw him a hard glance.

The temperature in the car park seemed even colder than before after the heat inside the club and Kate was shivering uncontrollably as she followed Horse to a big white Transit van parked under one of the car park's security lights. 'Have a seat,' he drawled, throwing the front passenger door open and striding around to the driver's side. This is madness, Kate thought – against all the rules that had been drummed into her – but nevertheless, she found herself climbing up into the van.

The joint was produced almost immediately from the glove compartment but she shook her head in a polite, though firm refusal. 'I don't do weed,' she snapped. 'It's crap.'

He nodded slowly. 'I don't think you *do* anything,' he replied, his tone suddenly grim.

She swallowed hard, trying to avoid the fierce gaze he turned on her and reaching for the door handle. 'I think I'll go back inside,' she said. 'It's cold out here.'

The arm that was thrown across her bare midriff as he reached for the door and hauled it shut seemed as hard as seasoned wood. 'Let's stop playing games, love, eh?' he snapped. 'You're no more a user than my old mum.'

'Let me out of here,' she gasped, struggling futilely as he held the door shut. 'You have no right—'

'Right?' he echoed. 'I've every right.'

And she gaped as he flashed a leather wallet in front of her eyes. The badge on one side and the small card in its plastic sheath on the other were unmistakable in the light from the overhead lamp standard. 'You're job?' she exclaimed.

He withdrew his arm and sat back in his seat, lighting his own joint and filling the car with the sweet nauseating smell of cannabis. 'Detective Constable Larry Gittings, National Crime Agency, love,' he said, 'or should I call you Mistress Plod?'

She shook her head in disbelief and produced her own warrant card. He barely glanced at it. 'Local Bill, are you then?' he queried.

'How the hell did you know?'

He emitted a disparaging laugh. 'Oh come on, love. I could smell you from the start – and more importantly, so could anyone else.'

'But – but what—?'

'Am I doing here?' He snorted. 'Well, I was working under-cover, if your antics tonight haven't put paid to that now.'

He turned towards her again and he looked angry. 'This operation has taken us a year to set up, do you know that? And I was getting so close. Then along comes some swede plod and puts her oar in to foul up the whole thing.'

She swallowed hard. Good on you, girl, she thought. Yet another own goal. You're doing well at the moment, aren't you?

'You could have let us know what was going on,' she snapped but as soon as she'd said it, she realized how stupid the words must have sounded.

He laughed again. 'Oh yeah, I could have just waltzed into your nick and had a meeting with everyone: "Hey, guys, my name's Horse and I'm with the NCA, doing a bit of undercover work at the Sapphire Club. So why don't you all mosey on down there and have a drink with me some time?" Something like that, eh?'

She clenched her teeth tightly. 'This isn't a joke. I'm

investigating a possible murder. This guy, Leroy, could be involved.'

He nodded again, stubbing out his cigarette on the dashboard. 'Well, you can tell me all about it in the morning, 'cause I plan to be in your nick to see your guv'nor first thing. Now get your trim little arse out of my wagon and go home. I think you've done enough damage for one night.'

Without warning, he swung on her again and with one movement ripped the front of her top apart. 'That should make our little tête-à-tête look a bit more kosher, if anyone's watching, eh?'

'You bastard!' she gasped and, scrambling out of his van, sprinted to her own car on the other side of the car park, holding the remnants of her top together with both hands as she ran.

And in the shadows almost within spitting distance of her car, another pair of eyes watched her drive away with a grim smile of satisfaction.

CHAPTER 8

ONCE AGAIN DI Roscoe's office was clouded with smoke, which ironically was good for Kate this time, despite her objections a few days before, because she was able to sit back a little more unobtrusively in a corner, avoiding the hard gazes cast in her direction by her boss. Having already been up most of the night, engaged in a monumental row with Hayden after she had arrived home with her torn top, Kate looked pale and drawn, her hands tightly locked in her lap.

Roscoe also looked tired but, surprisingly, there was no sign of the anger he had displayed the previous day. In fact, he seemed strangely subdued – his glances in her direction registering bitter disappointment rather than anything else as the lanky long-haired detective from the NCA put his case.

Larry Gittings – or 'Horse', as he had called himself – was a lot leaner than he had appeared to Kate at the Sapphire Club and she noted with some surprise the array of tattoos on his bare forearms extending up under the short sleeves of his shirt – even more just visible on his chest through a gap where a button had not been fastened properly. Maybe the NCA didn't have the same aversion to tattoos being displayed by their officers as provincial police forces, like Avon and Somerset did, she thought ruefully. But there again, undercover officers tended to be laws unto themselves and a few tattoos probably went a long way towards helping someone in his position fit into the high-risk twilight world in which he moved.

Conscious of her gaze on him, Horse threw her a brief glance of his own and she picked up the arrogant smirk in his dark eyes.

'The fact is,' Gittings finished, 'I am an undercover operative and my assignment is part of a major initiative to tackle serious organized crime throughout the UK.'

'Doing what exactly?' Roscoe queried.

'I can't tell you that. All I can say is that the people I am tracking are members of a major international crime syndicate, which has moved its original base from the Smoke to the sticks and has key links not only to this country but also Europe, the States and the Middle East. Drugs, people trafficking, money laundering, murder – you name it, they are involved in it. The ramifications of a successful undercover operation would be colossal and would eclipse anything we have achieved before.

'I have managed to penetrate almost to the heart of the organization and I am this close,' and he made a pincer sign with his finger and thumb, 'to nailing their Mr Big, so the last thing I need is for some naïve swede plod, like your DS here, to blunder into things and cock everything up.'

'I am not naïve, I do not blunder into things and I am not a "plod", Detective *Constable*,' Kate almost spat, remembering her ripped top, 'I am an experienced detective *sergeant* and I am pursuing a legitimate inquiry into a suspicious death.'

Gittings shrugged, unaffected by her emphasis on the difference between their two ranks. 'Whatever! The fact remains that your amateurish antics could have resulted in our whole operation being flushed down the toilet.'

'From what I've seen of you,' Kate threw back, angered by his insulting manner, 'you'd be perfectly at home down there!'

'Enough!' Roscoe rapped. 'This sort of sniping will get us nowhere.' He glared at each of them in turn, then stubbed out his cigarette on the edge of the desk and scowled directly at the NCA man. 'You claim to be an undercover copper. How do we know that? You could be any arsehole.'

Gittings stubbed out his own cigarette (not cannabis this time), reached into the back pocket of his designer threadbare jeans and produced the familiar black leather wallet, which he slammed on to Roscoe's desk in front of him. 'What's that then?' he said in a tone of pure aggression. 'Scotch mist?' The distinctive badge glinted in the sunlight filtering into the room.

'Watch your lip,' Roscoe rapped back, picking up the wallet and studying the warrant card in its plastic sleeve, then adding, 'I've never heard of an undercover copper carrying his warrant card on him.'

'I don't normally. Most of the time it's kept elsewhere, but on occasions I need to carry it to prove my bona fides – like now, for example.'

The DI grunted and tossed the wallet unceremoniously into the other's lap, narrowly avoiding pitching it on to the floor.

Gittings didn't bat an eyelid. 'If you want additional verification,' he said, returning the wallet to his pocket, 'give the Agency a ring on this number.' And he coolly leaned on the edge of the desk and wrote down what turned out to be a telephone number and a contact name on the top of a memo pad bearing Roscoe's elaborate doodles, then sat back with the same arrogant smirk on his face.

For reply, the DI leaned forward, chewing gum slowly, his gaze fixed on the other's bearded face. 'You can count on it,' he said. 'Now, let me tell you something, *Mister*. My sergeant here is not an amateur, any more than I am. She is a highly professional and experienced DS and I am a detective inspector, which makes me a senior officer to you, whichever soddin' squad or agency you belong to. And don't think you can come into my nick and dictate to me what this department does or does not do on our own manor. We'll give you breathing space, but only as long as I think it's necessary. Now piss off out of my nick!'

Gittings had a face on him like thunder as he grabbed his leather jacket from the back of the chair and headed for the door, but Kate's satisfaction was short-lived. The moment the NCA man had left, the DI turned on her, his eyes still smouldering. 'As for you, Lewis,' he snarled, 'you deliberately disobeyed my instructions, risked your neck again and made us look like the bloody Keystone Cops.'

'Sorry, Guv,' Kate said for the second time in twenty-four hours. 'I just thought—'

'Thought? *Thought?*' the DI all but choked. 'Don't *think*, Lewis, just do as you're bloody well told! One more slip-up like this and you'll be back on the street, wearing a funny hat. Got it? Now forget the bloody Sapphire Club business and everything to do with it and stick to the Ellie Landy drowning inquiry.'

'But there's a definite link between the two!' Kate protested, shooting to her feet. 'The facts speak for themselves.'

Roscoe lurched to his feet. 'There *are* no facts, Lewis, only bollocks! Don't you understand? All this murder thing is in your own imagination and since this investigation started, you've gone from one wild theory to another. First, you suggested Ellie Landy could have been stiffed by weirdo, Graham Snell, whom you suspected without any reason of being a sexual pervert, then by Ellie Landy's old man for revenge; now it's the boss of some London drugs cartel fingered by the NCA. Where will it all end? You going to put the chief constable's name in the frame next?'

'I never suggested Graham Snell or Rod Tolan had stiffed her,' Kate protested angrily. 'I just said they were possible suspects if her death turned out not to be accidental. But now I am convinced her death was murder—'

'A few bruises and torn fingernails don't add up to murder. We have *nothing*.'

'The pathologist seemed to think differently.'

'The pathologist was putting forward a theory,' Roscoe said heavily, 'and that was all. Even she wasn't prepared to commit herself. I repeat, we have *nothing*. But what we *have* got is an ongoing murder investigation in Cheddar, a serial rapist on the rampage in Bridgwater and a multiple stabbing in Wells – all of which have massive resource implications. What the force doesn't need right now is an accidental drowning elevated to the status of a bloody murder, which will then require yet more resources!'

But Kate stuck to her guns. 'So what about the name – the Sandman – we found written in the book in her room? Now we know he is a real person and a powerful villain under investigation by NCA. It's obvious Ellie got too close to him and he had her killed.'

'OK, maybe she *was* snooping on his activities – doesn't prove he had her murdered.'

'So what about the girl, Polly, I told you about before that arsehole came in to complain? Was she Scotch mist, like that dickhead's warrant card?'

He ignored her insubordination. 'You are asking me to take the word of some coke-head junkie?' he expostulated. 'She must have seen you coming. It doesn't take long for word to get out on the street. She probably met the press girl at some stage and when she heard she had snuffed it, made up this cock and bull story to squeeze some cash out of you – succeeded too, didn't she?' He took a deep breath. 'Ellie Landy drowned, do you understand the concept? She fell into the bloody river and drowned. End of!'

'So you're cuffing the whole thing?' she said, suspecting the influence of the DCI behind his decision. 'Bowing to internal politics and intimidation by Larry Gittings and the NCA?'

'I'm cuffing nothing,' Roscoe snarled, 'and you can get off your high horse, *madam*, and start doing what you should have been doing from the start – and that is getting out there, finding her missing car and wrapping this thing up, ready for the Coroner's Inquest. Is that clear enough for you?'

And he opened a thick buff file on his desk and began reading as if she were no longer there.

Angry, frustrated, but left with no other alternative, Kate stormed from the office and slammed the door hard behind her.

There was no one about in the vicinity of the pumping station when Kate drove up the bumpy track half an hour later. Why she had returned to the scene, she didn't really know herself. She'd just felt a strange inner compulsion to go back again, but once there she was at a loss what to do next.

The blue and white police tapes still fluttered under a faint breeze as she got out of the car and walked down the slope to the water's edge, starting involuntarily when a grey and white heron staggered skywards from a patch of reeds, panicked by her approach. Crouching on her haunches, she studied the flotsam still jammed into the bank, noting its regular rise and fall under the flow of the water, like the breast of a slate-grey beast whose lungs were constantly being inflated, then deflated by the action of a giant sub-merged diaphragm.

Straightening up with a shiver, she followed the now ragged curve of the river with her eyes, beyond the pumping station and the adjacent rhyne, until it was swallowed up in the patchwork of flooded fields stretching away into a hazy distance, wondering where on earth Ellie Landy might have gone into the water – and how it could have happened.

She glimpsed the khaki-coated figure as she was about to turn back towards her car. He was practically buried in a chest-high forest of tall yellow-plumed grass on the other side of the rhyne, close to the river's edge. Just his shoulders and the woolly hat he was wearing showing above it. It had started to rain – heavy drops that suggested an imminent downpour – and reason told her that her man was probably just fishing or bird-watching, but she was curious and decided to investigate; after all, it was also possible that he had been here before – the day Ellie Landy had drowned, for example.

A few yards behind the pumping station a narrow iron foot-bridge had been constructed across the rhyne and another barely discernible track struck out on the other side of it for a few yards before dwindling to nothing among the reeds and the flooded fields beyond. She used extreme care crossing the bridge, conscious of the dark water lapping the underside as she made her way down the slope towards the grass plumes, acutely conscious of the fact that, in her patent leather sling-backs, she was not exactly 'shod' for a tramp along a muddy river bank.

In fact, as it turned out, she didn't have that far to go, for her quarry emerged from the grass after she had only covered about two to three yards and he froze in the middle of the track, staring at her in astonishment.

She was equally surprised. 'Well, well, well, fancy meeting you here, as they say,' she commented drily. 'Doing a spot of fishing, are you, sir?'

Gabriel Lessing gave a nervous little laugh, playing with the lens of the camera slung over one shoulder. 'Just thought I'd – ah – take a look at the – ah – crime scene,' he said.

She frowned. 'What makes you think it is a crime scene?' she snapped.

He shrugged. 'Pretty obvious, isn't it? Fit young girl found drowned in a local river with a load of dodgy injuries. Has to be a murder.'

'Who says she had injuries?'

He tapped his nose, then abruptly went into a bout of familiar loose coughing. 'I have my sources,' he wheezed. 'Didn't do them herself, did she? And, according to her old man, it wasn't as though she couldn't swim either.'

'You've spoken to her father? How did you know where to find him?'

'Easy. I ain't a journalist for nothing.' Another grin. 'And seeing him was a story in itself. Knew who he was straightaway.'

'You have been busy,' she breathed.

He grinned. 'Someone has to be – and I intend being a lot more so too, since the police don't seem to be getting anywhere with the case.'

'There isn't a case,' she retorted, repeating what Roscoe had said to her. 'Ellie drowned. End of story.'

He shook his head. 'I don't think so, Sergeant. I reckon she was on to something big and someone took exception to it and wasted her.'

'And what would be this "big thing" be when it's at home?'

'I don't know yet, but I intend finding out.' He looked to be enjoying himself now. 'Drugs would be my guess. The slapper who ran out on you at the Toliver factory was obviously a junkie and what else would take you to the Sapphire Club, all dolled up in disco gear, but drugs?'

She froze. 'The Sapph—? Have you been following me?'

He chuckled. 'Didn't have a clue, did you, love? I just tailed you at a distance from the nick, then sat somewhere quiet like and watched. Very profitable bit of surveillance it was too.'

She made the connection suddenly and snapped her fingers. 'That was you at Toliver's, wasn't it? The loud noise that spooked her? You were trying to eavesdrop?'

He made a face. 'Yeah, bit careless there. Stepped on a sheet of asbestos. Couldn't get close enough before she scarpered. Pity.' He broke off, then said, 'So who was the big guy you had the argument with in the van at the club?'

She didn't volunteer a reply but took a step towards him. 'You sell any of this stuff for print and you're in big trouble, you piece of garbage.'

He raised his eyebrows. 'Ooh,' he mocked, 'that was a bit rude for a public servant – and I'm so scared.'

'You will be. You're in well over your head.'

He brushed past her towards the pumping station. 'Good hunting, Sarge,' he threw back at her over his shoulder. 'Be seeing you again.'

She watched his retreating figure with an angry scowl as he crossed the bridge and momentarily disappeared behind the pumping station before emerging a short distance beyond it, heading up the main track towards the road. Then she lost sight of him round a sharp bend and, as she headed back herself, she heard a vehicle start up and pull away. The pressman must have parked his car somewhere close by but she hadn't noticed it on the way in – probably hidden in a field behind a hedge. Pity he hadn't picked one that had been flooded, she thought vindictively as she looked around her at the submerged fields beyond the pumping station site. But one thing was certain; if the little jerk decided to file the story he had, Roscoe would be even less happy when he read his newspaper the following morning than he was at the moment. Suddenly the thought of the fortifying bottle of red wine nestling in the cupboard of the thatched cottage in Burtle village she and Hayden called home seemed much too good to ignore.

CHAPTER 9

ONE OF THE advantages of living within a relatively short distance of the job was that Kate and Hayden could unofficially nip home for lunch when they were not tied up on something, rather than use the small police station canteen, with its limited and normally pretty indigestible offerings. Doubly angry after her row with the DI and her bruising encounter with Gabriel Lessing, Kate bolted to the little thatched cottage in Burtle village straight after her confrontation with the newsman – and found Hayden already there, slouched in an armchair in the living room with an uncorked bottle of red wine on the coffee table in front of him and a plate of doorstep cheese sandwiches on his lap.

He seemed to have got over his anger of the previous night and he beamed at her as she stepped through the front door.

'Hi, Kate,' he said breezily. 'How did the meeting go?'

'Don't ask,' she snapped, dropping the ignition keys of her Mazda MX5 on the coffee table beside him. 'Saw the pool car parked outside. Bit of a sauce using a CID car to come home for lunch, wasn't it?'

He made a face. 'My Jag drinks too much petrol,' he said, as if that was a perfectly legitimate reason.

She grunted and went through to the kitchen to make some sandwiches for herself. 'Just don't let Roscoe catch you,' she said. 'He'll flay you alive.'

Hayden chuckled. 'Put him in a bad mood, did you, old girl?'

The response from the kitchen was sharp. 'Don't wind me up anymore.'

'You shouldn't have been such a naughty girl last night – your undercover man from NCA there, was he?'

'You bet he was and he certainly got Roscoe all hot and bothered.'

'That must have been worth seeing.'

There was silence for a couple of minutes and then she reappeared with a much thinner double sandwich and an empty wine glass. 'The long and the short of it is we're banned from going anywhere near the Sapphire Club in future and the DI's now decided to cuff the bloody drowning as well,' she said, taking his bottle and pouring herself a large measure. 'Wants it wrapped up as an accident – like yesterday.'

Hayden nodded, waving half a sandwich in one hand as he spoke through a mouthful of bread and cheese. 'I could see that coming from day one with everything that's going on at the moment,' he replied. 'There are only four of us left in the department now and he wouldn't be flavour of the month if he called for another major crime investigation to be set up.'

She nibbled a corner of her sandwich, then set the plate down on the arm of the settee, suddenly no longer hungry. 'So we just bury a murder then and that's OK, is it?'

He stared at her. 'That's a bit harsh, isn't it? Poor old Ted Roscoe is between a rock and a hard place on this one. If he says "accident", someone like you will shout "foul" and if he says "murder", the powers that be will scream "where's your evidence?" He can't win.'

'Sounds like you're on his side? You forget the pathologist's findings and the girl, Polly.'

He shrugged. 'One so-called expert's opinion, coupled with the word of a junkie who has only been seen by you and has now disappeared—'

'You *are* on Roscoe's side.'

He spat crumbs across the coffee table. 'Oh come on,

Kate, get real. We've got a sus death, I'll give you that, but we haven't enough to positively label it a murder. And, don't forget, we're still waiting on the pathologist's other tests – toxicology and so forth.'

'Even a sus death should be fully investigated, as you well know, and just because we are short on troops, does that justify cuffing the whole thing?'

How Hayden would have got out of that one, it is impossible to say, for he didn't even get to open his mouth before the house phone shrilled. Frowning, Kate lifted it from its cradle on the shelf behind her.

'Thought I'd find you there,' Roscoe rapped. 'Fish and chips at home with hubby, is it?'

'Cheese sandwiches actually, Guv,' Kate responded coldly. 'We're allowed a meal break—'

'Never mind that,' the DI cut in. 'Get your arses down to the hospital. They've got a DOA – believed OD on heroin. And by the way, doc says it is definitely an OD – nothing suspicious, right? So try not to see this as yet another murder, Lewis!'

On arrival at the hospital mortuary, however, Kate couldn't help herself, for the emaciated girl lying on the gurney in front of one of the fridges was none other than her junkie informant, Polly!

Hayden was losing patience. 'Kate, it was an overdose,' he exclaimed, his exasperation showing. 'She had tramlines on both arms and both legs and a dirty syringe still in her arm, for goodness' sake!'

Kate rounded on her husband in the hospital car park, shock still evident on her face. 'You just don't get it, do you, Hayd?' she shouted. 'None of you do. *You* saw the name in the book at Ellie Landy's lodgings – Sandman? He's a real person, not some figment of my imagination. Polly told me he killed Ellie and she herself was running from one of his thugs. Now she's dead too. OD? Yeah, maybe, but not by her hand, I'll bet my career on it.'

He sighed. 'You might have to, old thing,' he said quietly, 'if Roscoe hears you come out with any of this.'

'This is not about Roscoe,' she said bitterly. 'It's Ricketts – the DCI – looking for a bloody quiet life. Roscoe's being leaned on – it's all sodding politics – you know that. I just can't believe that tough, old, no-nonsense bastard is going along with it.'

Kate turned her back on him and marched to the CID car he was driving, slamming into the front passenger seat in a cold frustrated rage as he slipped behind the wheel.

'So, where to now?' he queried gently.

Kate glared at him. 'You *know* where to, Hayd,' she grated, 'or weren't you bloody listening? Paramedic said she was found in an old canal boat moored on the Bridgwater Canal, so that's where to. OK? All we have to do is look for a flashing blue light on the sodding towpath. Think you can manage that?'

But Hayden knew better than to answer when she was in this kind of mood and simply started the engine and reversed out of the parking bay, heading for the exit.

There was no blue light flashing. The driver of the patrol car had no doubt switched it off to save the battery, but the police car wasn't difficult to pick out. A middle-aged policewoman walked over to them when they pulled up behind it and nodded unnecessarily towards the solitary green and black houseboat moored close to the canal bank just feet away.

'Need to be careful,' the policewoman warned. 'The boat's pretty low in the water and some of the decking is rotten. Apparently it was condemned over three months ago.'

Kate grunted. 'Poor little cow,' she murmured. 'How was she found?'

'Dog walker,' the constable replied. 'Saw her sprawled on

the deck and did a three nines on his mobile. She was still alive – just – but apparently snuffed it on the way to hospital.'

Hayden – ever the gentleman – preceded Kate on to the boat's creaking for'ard deck to test its strength before reaching down to help her over the gap between the bank and the hull. She ignored his proffered hand and pushed past him to a flight of wooden steps leading below.

The place stank. Body odour mixed with the dank smell of the canal, which was only just visible through dirty cracked windows. Clothes were piled everywhere in untidy heaps and an unfinished ready-meal in a foil tray stood on the pull-out table amid a litter of needles, joints and dirty paper tissues.

'Poor little cow,' Kate said again.

'Where do we start looking?' Hayden queried cheerfully, though the disagreeable look on his face was at a complete variance with his tone.

Kate shrugged. 'You do the cupboards to the right and I'll do those on the left,' she said, indicating the rows of small sliding doors close to the floor.

'Starboard for me and port for you then?' Hayden drawled in his most superior voice. 'What are we looking for?'

Kate gave him an old-fashioned look. 'I haven't the faintest,' she retorted and crouched down to start the search on her side, sliding each door back with the care of someone expecting something unpleasant – like a poisonous spider – to leap out at her.

There were no poisonous spiders, however, and she found nothing else out of the ordinary either – just a few tins of food, mainly baked beans, a few empty wine bottles and some stained underclothes, and it was actually Hayden who came up with 'the goods' in the end, bringing her to her feet in a rush when he exclaimed, 'What's this then?'

The A4 size piece of stiff, once glossy paper had been folded into four and was torn and dirty but the printing, superimposed on a coloured picture of a dance in full swing, was clear enough to read and Kate snatched what was plainly an advertisement poster from his hand before he could comment further.

'The Sapphire Club,' she said aloud, scanning the invitation to attend one of its gigs for the 'bargain price' of fifteen pounds. 'Couple of months ago, going by the date.'

Hayden nodded. 'But that isn't the interesting bit,' he said. 'Turn it over.'

She did so and started. Someone, presumably the dead girl, had used the back of one folded section of the poster to write down a name and what appeared to be a mobile telephone number in a felt tip pen – and the name jumped right out at her. '"Leroy",' she breathed.

'Otherwise known as the Spliff,' he finished for her.

'At last we have a definite link,' she said, and her eyes were shining.

'For all the good it will do us,' he replied, 'since we can't go anywhere near the club anyway.'

'Maybe not,' she agreed, producing her mobile phone, 'but there's nothing to stop us dialling a telephone number is there?'

At first Kate thought there was no one at home when she rang, but then the mobile at the other end rasped and a gruff voice said, 'Yeah?'

'Leroy?' Kate queried, keeping her voice low.

'Who wanna' know?'

Kate took a chance. 'Sally – friend of a friend.'

'What friend?'

'Polly.'

There was silence for a moment. Then the voice grunted, 'Don't know no Polly.'

'Polly said you could help me with some stuff.'

'Stuff? Don't know what yo' mean.'

'Said you had some good jenny.'

'Jenny? What yo' talkin' about – yo' mad person?'

She manufactured a gasp. 'Listen, I'm really jonesing for some stuff. Polly said to call you.'

'Hey, you got wrong number, girl. Can't help you with noffink.'

'I've got fifty says you would like to.'

There was a disparaging snort, but then greed overruled caution. 'Need more'n fifty – less you is a jolly pop?'

'I ain't no jolly pop, but fifty's all I got.'

Leroy thought about that a bit longer. Kate could practically hear the cogs in his brain turning. 'Why yo' come to me now? Ain't never heard of no Sally before neiv'er.'

'Just got in from the Smoke. Used to live around here.'

He gave a non-committal grunt. 'Yo' better be legit or I cut yo' bad.' Kate didn't answer and he belched. 'Yo know ol' Toliver factory near Street?'

She remembered her meeting with Polly and her mouth tightened.

'Yeah, I know it.'

'Be there at four. What you look like?'

'Ginger hair, black leather coat.'

'Cool.'

'How will I know you?'

But there was no answer and Kate swore as the line abruptly went dead. Then she looked up to see Hayden staring at her.

'What the devil was all that about?' he exclaimed. 'And where did you learn all that gibberish? Jenny, jonesing, jolly pop – it was as if you were on another planet.'

She gave a short laugh. 'Ah, but there you are, my man, I have hidden depths, you see.' Then she was serious again. 'Nine months attached to Drug Squad actually.'

He frowned. 'Oh yes, I remember – that big operation in Bristol. So what did it all mean, Miss Clever Dick?'

She shrugged. 'Well, jenny is heroin, jonesing means I

94

need it really badly and jolly pop is someone who is not really an addict, but just a casual user, who wouldn't need much of a score.'

He grunted. 'I'm impressed. But you're not meeting with a creep like him on your own and that's final! It's much too dangerous.'

She cast him a mischievous sideways glance. 'I wasn't intending to. I thought you'd be coming with me.'

'Me?' He coughed, clearly not expecting this kind of conciliatory reaction from her or to find himself so easily out-manoeuvred. 'But – but, yes, of course. Good idea. So – er – what's our strategy then?'

'Strategy?'

He sighed his irritation. 'Well, you've set up this meet, so you must have some idea what you are going to do when our man turns up?'

She shrugged. 'I thought that as soon as he produced the goods, we'd nick him for possession with intent to supply and, once we'd got him inside, we'd be in a position to interrogate him about Ellie Landy's death.'

He pursed his lips in a low whistle. 'I never realized my wife could be so devious – Roscoe will do his crust, you know that, don't you?'

'He can spit and fart all he likes, but he can hardly criticize us for nicking a pusher.'

Hayden nodded, then looked suddenly dubious. 'Chap could have a blade – or worse – on him. We should arrange for backup, just in case.'

She shook her head firmly. 'No way. First sign of a plod and he'll be on his toes.'

'You're putting a lot on me.'

She smiled thinly and, reaching into her coat pocket, produced a small metal cylinder. 'But I also have this.'

He gaped. 'CS? Are you mad?'

Another shrug. 'Not as far as I know. They're official issue, aren't they?'

He stared at her in disbelief. 'Yes, but only for use in exceptional circumstances. Roscoe would blow a gasket if he knew what you were at.'

She returned the gas spray to her pocket with a soft chuckle. 'Well, I won't tell him if you don't,' she said.

CHAPTER 10

TOLIVER'S SEEMED JUST as deserted as before – even the tortoiseshell cat was nowhere to be seen – and it was raining heavily when Kate and Hayden pulled up outside. They were an hour early – hopefully getting there well before Leroy, who they guessed would turn up at least half an hour before the appointed time, to ensure the meeting wasn't some kind of a trap.

A strengthening wind was driving the rain almost horizontally across the concrete apron as they ran for the loading bay entrance and the building breathed a death rattle welcome, its whole fabric shaking and a door banging with a steady 'thump, thump, thump' somewhere deep inside as they flicked on their torches to probe the gloomy interior which lay beyond the reach of the grey light filtering through the skylights.

Kate selected a spot close to the door through which Polly had made both her entrance and her exit, leaning against the wall, while Hayden found a convenient space behind a couple of massive steel drums and settled himself on a pile of sacks to await developments.

It proved to be a long wait too, and Kate soon came off her wall and began shuffling up and down in an effort to cope with the bitter cold that was seeping into her bones from the concrete floor. At the same time, however, she showed little sympathy for Hayden in his confined hiding place; glaring in his direction and issuing a sharp hiss every time his heels scraped the floor, as he shifted his cramped limbs into a more comfortable position.

But, after what seemed like an eternity, the sound of an approaching car became audible and Kate tensed as the engine died outside the factory. A strained silence followed. No door slammed, no footsteps crunched on the loading bay floor; there was nothing save the sporadic whistle of the wind and the rattle of the rain on the corrugated iron roof. If the new arrival *was* Leroy, he seemed to be in no immediate hurry to join them – probably studying the building for any sign of a reception committee.

In fact, the dark figure emerged from the mouth of the loading bay without warning, rubber-soled shoes making no sound on the floor as it picked its way carefully into view, the beam of a small torch masked in one hand.

Kate tensed and stepped away from the wall to face the new arrival. 'Leroy?' she queried, her quivering voice and shivers not entirely manufactured, and coincidentally adding substance to the part she was playing as an addict desperate for her next fix.

'Yo' Sally?' he responded, coming closer.

In the grey light penetrating the place through the sky-lights she saw that he was a black man she judged to be in his late twenties or early thirties, dressed in a brown hooded coat and blue jeans. He was carrying a holdall and Kate caught the glimpse of gold on his wrist as he raised one arm to wipe his nose on the back of his hand.

'Got the bread?' he said.

'See the stuff first.'

Leroy shook his head. 'Don't work like that, babe.' He held out his free hand and rubbed the fingers together. 'Loot, now or I split.'

Kate's body convulsed in an involuntary shudder and Leroy laughed. 'Yo' got it bad, babe,' he mocked. 'Yo' need jenny more'n I need bread.'

98

What Kate would have done next stayed a mystery, for it was at this point that Hayden chose to – quite literally – put his big size elevens in it. Seized by a sudden spasm of severe cramp, he carefully moved his leg, but not quite carefully enough and the next instant he caught one of the drums he was sheltering behind with his heel. The reverberating bang had a dramatic effect on the dynamics of the situation. Jerking his head round briefly in the direction of the sound, Leroy lunged at Kate, with a narrow-bladed knife in his hand.

'Bitch!' he snarled – a second before the explosive hiss of Kate's CS gas spray brought him to his knees, gagging, retching and clawing at his eyes in agony, the knife clattering to the concrete floor, as his temporarily paralysed diaphragm shut down his respiratory system.

Before he could fully recover, Hayden was on to him, his heavy frame crushing Leroy face downwards against the concrete floor. 'I think the phrase is, "you're nicked",' the detective said close to his ear as he whipped a pair of handcuffs from his pocket.

Leroy ignored the mug of coffee on the table in front of him and seemed more interested in the antics of a heavyweight fly which had become trapped in the interview room and was now head-banging the closed window. Kate and Hayden sat silently in their chairs on the opposite side of the desk, waiting patiently for him to answer the question Kate had just put to him.

The vicious little pusher showed no inclination to answer, however, and as the minutes ticked by, Kate finally broke the silence. 'I asked you where you got the heroin,' she said.

Leroy turned and stared her out. 'Got noffink to say, bitch,' he replied and waved a hand towards the tape machine in the corner behind him, which was recording the interview with a delicate humming sound. ''Cept yo' be sorry for settin' me up, 'cause I gonna sue that tight little arse off.'

'Bit difficult trying to do that from stir,' Hayden commented drily, 'especially if you're on a six-year stretch for supplying.'

Leroy tensed and the dark eyes that swung on Hayden radiated pure hate. 'Yo' got big mouth, fat man,' he snarled. 'An' I got a long memory for what yo' done.' He pointed to the still raw abrasion and heavy bruising to one side of his face. 'I don't never forget.'

'Good,' Kate continued. 'So maybe you can tell us where you got the heroin. You're banged to rights on this one and your only way out is to co-operate with us.'

Leroy snorted. 'Get real, bitch!' he spat. 'Help the *PO*-lice? I like breav'in' too much.'

'So did Polly and Ellie Landy,' Kate said grimly, studying his face.

She was rewarded by a definite narrowing of Leroy's eyes. 'Dunno what yo' on about,' he replied and, like the politician on television who reaches for a glass of water when presented with a difficult question, he picked up his mug of coffee and took his time sipping it.

'I think you know exactly what I'm on about.'

'Don't know no Ellie Landy.'

'But you knew Polly?'

'Maybe I did, maybe I didn't.'

'Did you waste her?' Hayden said abruptly.

Leroy didn't bat an eyelid, showing no surprise at the revelation that she was dead or any sense of indignation that he was being accused.

'Don't waste nobody, man. I a businessman. Ain't no killer.'

'Just pumped a bit too much H into her veins, did you?' Hayden persisted. 'A nice mind-blowing overdose to shut her up? Now, that's not a six-year stretch – that's life!'

For the first time Leroy looked uneasy and his eyes flicked from Hayden to Kate, like a cornered animal. 'You ain't got noffink on me. I weren't nowhere near her bloody boat.'

'How did you know she died on a boat?' Hayden went on, leaning forward across the table towards him.

Leroy swallowed hard. 'Yo tol' me.'

'I said she likely died of an overdose. I didn't say where.'

Leroy was really agitated now. 'I want a brief. Yo can't ask me all these fings wiv'out a brief.'

'Someone put you up to the job, did they?' Kate said, ignoring his demand. 'Who was it, Leroy? The guy who fixes you up with the stuff for your punters?'

Leroy shook his head several times and there was a flicker of fear in his eyes this time. 'I ain't sayin' noffink wiv'out a brief. Yo savvy?'

Whether the detectives would have persisted with their questions, regardless of the legal constraints on the interviewing of suspects, was not put to the test, for at this point the process was rudely interrupted by Ted Roscoe, who suddenly burst into the room with the force of a JCB, his slab-like face set in a ferocious scowl.

'DI Ted Roscoe entering the room,' he announced for the benefit of the recording machine. 'Interview suspended at 1730 hours.'

Crossing to the tape machine, he switched it off and turned on Kate, his boot-button eyes boring into her like twin lasers. 'My office, Sergeant,' he snapped. '*Now*, if you please. And for the moment, you can lodge Leroy here in the detention room. I'm sure he hasn't any other pressing appointments!'

Kate was hit by a mixture of surprise and apprehension when she finally pushed through the main doors of the CID department and was momentarily confronted by 'Horse' coming out.

'Sergeant,' the NCA man acknowledged, easing past her, and there was a contemptuous sneer on his face as he added, 'You've really excelled yourself this time, haven't you?'

Roscoe was pacing his inner sanctum at the far end of the big open-plan office and he glared at her when she entered his domain after a brief knock, his head thrust forward in a familiar, belligerent fashion and the veins standing out like tight blue cords on both sides of his forehead.

'What did I order you *not* to do?' he demanded and drew heavily on a cigarette as he waited for a reply.

Choosing not to remind him again about the smoking ban, for fear of winding him up even more, Kate answered, 'Go anywhere near the Sapphire Club, and I didn't.'

He snorted. 'I told you to concentrate on the Ellie Landy inquiry and forget about everything else – so what do you do? You stick your nose into the same business I specifically ordered you to leave alone.'

Kate met his gaze without flinching. 'With respect, *sir*, I had no choice. The girl, Polly, was found dead on a canal boat and I was sent to deal with the job.'

He shook his head. 'Then why have I got some bloody pusher from the Sapphire Club in my bloody nick, as a result, eh?'

So Kate told him, her tone brittle and uncompromising, and he threw his hands up in the air in a gesture of despair, smoke trailing from the cigarette between two fingers.

'Not this bloody murder conspiracy all over again. You need to see a shrink – OCD, they call it, Obsessive Compulsive Disorder.'

'This is no joke, Guv,' she snapped.

'Do you see me laughing?' he retorted, stubbing out the cigarette on the desk top. 'Or your mate, Horse? According to him, this Leroy character has close links with the syndicate he has been investigating, so he was not in the least bit amused to find him banged up here. I doubt whether his commander will see the funny side of things either if, by nicking the little toe-rag and taking him off the street, we sever that link and foul up the whole NCA operation.'

Kate was ahead of him now and she gaped. 'You're not going to chuck him out, are you?'

He shrugged, weary now rather than angry. 'I've already instructed the custody sergeant to release him on police bail. That gives your mate, Horse, a month's grace to tie things up before his man has to report back here, following a final decision by CPS.'

'But he's a dealer – he tried to sell me heroin!'

'Yeah,' he agreed, 'after you had set him up. How do you think that will go down in court? It'll be the same old agent provocateur defence these bastards always use and he will walk, believe me.'

She shook her head desperately. 'I can't believe I'm hearing this. We're just an hour or so away from getting a cough and we just dump the one chance we have.'

He snorted. 'A cough? A cough to what? We don't have anything he can cough to – except being a dealer. Forget it, Lewis. Get with the real world – and this is your last warning.' He waggled a short stubby finger. 'No more private adventures, OK? And I mean it. Stay with reality.'

She took a deep breath and nodded. 'Fine but I'm really disappointed. I thought you were the bee's knees as a DI. Seems I was wrong.'

'Piss off!' he grated.

'With pleasure, *sir*,' she replied and walked out.

'Are you mad?' Hayden stared at Kate in open-mouthed astonishment. 'How many warnings do you need?'

Back at their thatched cottage in the village of Burtle, the pair had finished a meal of steak and chips and they were already on to their second bottle of red wine.

Kate, clad in just a knee-length cotton nightdress, stretched on the settee beside her husband and studied him in his striped boxer shorts and T-shirt. 'You don't understand,' she said defensively. 'I can't just let this thing go. You know as well as I do that both girls were murdered. We have to get to the bottom of this business. We owe it to them, if nothing else.'

Hayden refilled his glass from the newly opened bottle and sighed. 'We *know* nothing of the sort, old girl,' he replied. 'We only suspect something dodgy. We can't *prove* anything and our last lead died with that Polly girl.'

'So we try a different approach.'

Hayden eyed her long slender legs, then locked on to an expanse of bare thigh that her rucked-up nightdress had now exposed. 'Er – like what?' he queried, taking a quick gulp of his wine.

Kate cast him a mischievous smile. 'Will you stop undressing me with your eyes?' she said.

He looked away, staring into the spluttering open fire. 'Not much left to undress, is there?' he retorted, then quickly changed the subject. 'You were saying we try a different approach?'

She nodded, suddenly serious again. 'We find out where Ellie Landy went into the water, which neither Roscoe or Horse can object to – after all, it's a logical step for us to take in our inquiries.'

He frowned. 'And how do you expect to do that? She could have gone in anywhere.'

Kate shrugged, returning her half-full wine glass to the coffee table in front of her. 'By a bit of old-fashioned legwork,' she replied. 'We get some pics run off from her press card then show them to folk living near where the body was found – see if we can get any positive sightings. There's a farm and a collection of cottages a few hundred yards from the pumping station, so that would be a good place to start.'

'So why haven't these "folk" contacted us already? The drowning has been in all the papers, on radio and TV. Someone would have been in touch long before now if they were going to be in touch at all.'

Kate shook her head. 'Not necessarily. Maybe they don't take a newspaper or just didn't want to get involved in the first place?'

'Unlikely – and if they didn't want to get involved at the start, how do we get them to spill the beans to us now?'

Kate stretched even more and rubbed one bare foot along his leg. 'By using all our natural charm and chemistry,' she said, exposing even more thigh. 'And since I plan to make a start first thing in the morning, it might be a good idea to get an early night.'

Hayden grinned broadly. 'I'll drink to that,' he exclaimed enthusiastically.

Kate chuckled. 'Drinking isn't really what I had in mind,' she said.

CHAPTER 11

THE FIRST PART of Kate's 'brilliant new plan' was an immediate success. Photocopying Ellie Landy's photograph on her press card and producing a bundle of enlarged pictures was accomplished within an hour and getting out to the scene took just half an hour more. But the second part of the plan proved more problematical. The weather was the principal factor. Vast tracts of the countryside were still flooded several feet deep and Kate soon discovered that even her knee-length leather boots would have been of little benefit in the deep water.

After visiting half a dozen accessible properties and one isolated inn, they were halted by what resembled an inland sea of murky, grey water, traversed by a criss-cross pattern of drowned trees and hedgerows, where the lower moor stretched away to a misty horizon and the slight hump of the marooned village of Lowmoor.

For a moment Hayden just stood there in his Parka and gumboots, shoulders hunched against the driving rain, staring down at the water lapping the foot of the slope in front of them. 'Gordon Bennett, this is futile,' he shouted above the sound of the rain, anger evident in his tone but, true to form, refusing to resort to the usual expletives others might have used in such circumstances. 'We're getting nowhere.'

Kate tightened the cord strap of her black anorak under her chin and chuckled, turning towards him. 'Poor old Hayd,' she said loudly. 'Don't like the rain, do you, my love?'

He snorted. 'They say a good copper never gets wet,' he retorted, 'and I'm drenched – all for nothing.'

'Not nothing,' she corrected, waving an arm towards a couple of the cottages that lined one side of the lane in which they had parked the car. 'We've eliminated a few possible witnesses anyway.'

'So can we go back to the nick for a break?' he queried. 'Or – better still – home, to dry off?'

She shook her head. 'There are still a few properties to be checked.'

'We can always come back afterwards?'

Kate shook her head. 'We need to keep going.'

'Even though we're likely to catch pneumonia?'

She laughed again. 'A cop's got to do what a cop's got to do,' she retorted in her worst American accent.

But, as it turned out, Hayden was to be relieved of the responsibility. Even as he opened his mouth with a further objection, his police radio activated. It was the control room and Kate's irritation was apparent as he acknowledged the call with an apologetic glance in her direction.

'Job for you, Hayden,' the operator informed him. 'Burglary at a house in Mark village.'

'Committed on the Levels,' he replied. 'Can you send another unit?'

'Uniform tied up and no other CID units available,' came the almost gleeful 'you can't get out of this one'.

'Shit!' Kate exclaimed once he was off air.

He grinned through the rain. 'Time to go then?' he said hopefully.

'For you, yes,' she agreed. 'Take the car and sort this job out. I'll call up when I'm done here and want collecting again.'

'Not a chance,' he said defiantly. 'I'm not leaving you out here on your own – you could end up like Ellie Landy.'

'Bollocks!' she blazed. 'Now, I'm giving you an order. Get your arse in gear and over to Mark.'

And to reinforce the point, she produced her car keys and slapped them in his hand. 'Go!' she snapped. 'I mean it, Hayd. Piss off!'

A few seconds longer he hesitated, but the rain suddenly increasing in its intensity soon made up his mind and, with a rueful wave, he stomped back up the lane to where they had left the car. 'Watch yourself,' he threw back over his shoulder, 'and don't talk to any strange men!'

Kate had good cause to remember her husband's parting shot when she knocked on the door of the redbrick cottage fifteen minutes later. The cottage was at the far end of the lane – set apart from the rest, with a rubber dinghy equipped with an outboard motor on a trailer in the front garden – and it was the last of the remaining four properties she had tasked herself to check out. The other three had proved to be a waste of time – the first being empty and the other two occupied by elderly residents who could hardly remember what day it was, let alone recall whether they had ever clapped eyes on Ellie Landy. The young man who came to the door of the red-brick cottage in answer to her knock was an entirely different proposition, however. In his late twenties or early thirties, with lank blond shoulder-length hair, a pasty pock-marked face and thin stooped frame, he radiated strangeness and his sullen hostility was palpable as soon as Kate produced her warrant card.

'And what do *you* want?' he muttered, avoiding her gaze and staring down at his feet.

Kate stiffened, picking up the bad vibes immediately. 'We are making inquiries into the death of this young woman and wondered whether you have ever seen her before,' she said, holding Ellie Landy's photograph up in front of him. 'Her name was Ellie Landy and she was found drowned in the River Parrett near here a few days ago. You may have read about the incident in the newspapers or seen it on local TV?'

'No, I haven't,' he replied tersely and made to close the door again.

Kate put her foot on the sill, sensing that something was very wrong. 'Do you mean you haven't seen her before or you haven't read the story in the newspapers?' she persisted.

There was venom in his expression now. 'Both,' he said, his pale blue eyes flicking to her face and back to his feet again.

'But you haven't really looked at the photograph?'

'Haven't seen her, all right?' he snapped and tried to close the door again.

Before he could, however, another figure appeared at his elbow. 'Who is it, Sam?' the stout elderly woman demanded, peering round him to give Kate the once-over.

'Police,' Sam replied, still in a mutter.

The woman pushed past him. 'What's my son done now?' she snapped, suddenly equally hostile.

Kate frowned. 'Nothing as far as I know,' she said and quickly explained the reason for her visit.

The woman took a deep breath and stared at the young man. 'I said you should have reported it,' she exclaimed.

'Be quiet, Mother!' he snapped, glaring at her.

'Reported what?' Kate queried.

The woman stepped forward, pushing him to one side. 'The Landy woman,' she replied, ignoring her son's angry stare. 'I told him to tell the police about her, but he was frightened he might end up in trouble again.'

Kate sighed. 'Look,' she said, 'can I come in? I think we need to talk.'

The woman pushed Sam out of the way and stepped to one side. 'Please do,' she invited.

Sitting at the kitchen table a few moments later, Kate spread her hands out on the table top. 'So, what have you got to tell me?' she said.

The elderly woman took a deep breath. 'Sam has been in trouble,' she explained, throwing her son a troubled glance as he leaned against the sink, arms folded, his gaze fixed sullenly on the tiled floor. 'He has these urges, you see. And he was put away for indecently assaulting two young women two years ago. He has only been out six months, so you can understand why he doesn't want anything to do with the police – he's scared that he might be accused of something—'

Kate cut her off with a wave of her hand. 'I'm not interested in his previous,' she said, 'only in what he has to tell me about the girl in this photograph.'

She held it up in front of her and the woman compressed her lips into a hard line, then nodded quickly, throwing another brief glance at her son before continuing. 'Sam has the boat that's parked out front, you see,' she explained. 'He's into all sorts of adventure sports and takes it all over the country. Anyway, a few days ago, this young woman turned up in a flashy sports car, knocked on the door and asked Sam if she could hire it—'

'Hire it?'

'Yes, she wanted to get to Lowmoor for some reason and had missed the morning boat that regularly takes supplies and so forth into the village. She offered to pay Sam a lot of money if he would do it, so he agreed and took her across there that same day. He never saw her again, did you Sam?'

She glanced back at her son for a moment, but he made no response, continuing to stare down at his feet in an apparent bad-tempered sulk.

Kate raised her head to study him. 'Well, did you, Sam?' she repeated. 'Or have we got to continue this discussion down at the police station?'

The boy stiffened and raised his head to meet her stare.

'Never touched her, if that's what you mean,' he said. 'Just dropped her off and came back, I – I swear it.'

'No one is suggesting you touched her, Sam,' she said, more gently this time, 'but was the girl the one in this photograph?'

He gave a reluctant nod.

'Did she say why she wanted to get to Lowmoor?'

He shook his head. 'Just said she needed to get there.'

'And you weren't curious as to why?'

He gave a faint grin. 'Gave me thirty quid, so why would I care?'

Kate sighed. 'Your mum said the woman turned up in a flashy sports car. Where's the car now?'

Sam hesitated, then stood up. 'I'll show you.'

The car was an old, but apparently restored MGB and it was parked in an open barn a few yards past the cottage. The car was securely locked and glistening with damp – a glance through a side window was enough for Kate. There was an open Ordinance Survey map, stained with the remains of a leaking sandwich, on the passenger seat and several business cards stuck to the sticky deposit that the sandwich had left. The bold black heading at the top of one of the cards read 'Lessings Global News Agency' and the name 'Ellie Landy' printed below it was easily legible.

'You just left it here?' she queried.

'What was I supposed to do with it?' he said sullenly. 'Weren't my car and she had the keys anyway.'

Kate nodded slowly. 'OK, Sam, thanks for your help. Now, can I borrow your boat for a couple of hours?'

He started, then firmly shook his head. 'I don't loan it out,' he replied. 'It's the bee's knees – electric start, full auto–choke and electric fuel pump. Cost me a bundle.'

Kate reached under her coat and thrust her hand into her back pocket, pulling out her wallet. 'I'll make it worth your while,' she said and withdrew several notes and placed them on the bonnet of the car in front of him. His eyes fastened on the money, but he still shook his head.

'I'll take you there,' he offered, 'but I won't loan you my dinghy.'

Kate's mouth tightened. She was fast losing what little patience she had. 'I need to take myself over there,' she said.

'I have to be able to get back when I've finished what I've got to do and I don't know how long that will be.'

'No deal,' he said stubbornly.

Her eyes glittered. 'Then I'll have to requisition it,' she said, not sure whether she had the power to do anything of the sort. 'This is a police inquiry and I am going to borrow your boat whether you want me to or not. The money still stands, but I'm afraid you have no choice in the matter.'

Sam threw a desperate glance past her at his mother, who had followed them out to the barn and now stood in the doorway. She simply shrugged. 'As the officer's told you,' she said, 'you don't have a choice.'

Sam scowled. 'You bring her back safe,' he said. 'Anything happens to her, it'll cost you plenty.'

Kate treated him to her best smile. 'I promise,' she said, then spoiled it all by adding, 'Now, you'd better show me how the thing works!'

In fact, the dinghy proved surprisingly easy to handle. Five minutes instruction by a very apprehensive Sam, after he had wheeled the boat down to the water's edge, was enough and Kate left him with a swirl of water and a confident wave of her hand – which actually belied the apprehension she felt in relation to her debut 'sailing' expedition. Despite the rain and the ever-present threat of concealed hazards, like submerged cars, and the disappearance of the fences and hedgerows marking the road edges, she made it to the marooned village without mishap and killed the engine. Then, hauling the dinghy out of the water and well up on to the grass beside the road, she headed for the row of cottages lining both sides of what had once been the main street. At first she was heartened by the warm glow spilling out of some of the windows into the gradually departing daylight, but her optimism soon faded when she received no answer to her knocks from any of the cottages, even though the curtains across one window did stir, suggesting someone was inside.

The gloom of the day, worsened by the driving rain and emerging spirals of white mist, pressed in on her as she clomped up the narrow street towards the village centre, struck, in spite of the appalling weather, by the fact that the place seemed so deserted. Where was everyone? She felt a bit like the sheriff in the Western film, *High Noon*, sensing hidden eyes studying her from behind the closed windows as she walked on. The gently swinging inn sign was a welcome sight and she turned into the half-open door of the public bar with a sense of relief.

A dying fire burned through the mound of grey ash in the big open grate and several pairs of eyes homed in on her from dark corners as she crossed the bare wooden floor, conscious of the crack of her leather boots on the polished wood.

The buxom woman behind the bar smoothed her peroxide-dyed curls away from her face and forced a smile, which didn't reach her wary blue eyes. 'What'll you have, my duck?' she queried in a strong Somerset accent. 'Got a nice choice o'cider, if tha's to your likin' – local too. Good ol' Zomerset.'

Kate smiled, turning her head briefly to nod at a couple of rough labouring types occupying the end of the bar on red-leather cushioned stools. 'I'll take a half of whatever you would recommend,' she said in her most conciliatory tone.

The woman behind the bar nodded and grabbed a glass from the shelf behind her and thrust it under a pump. 'You're not from round 'ere,' she said, more as a statement than a question. 'Reckon I knows everyone in Lowmoor.'

Kate shook her head. 'First time.'

A frown greeted her answer. ''Ow you get 'ere then? We's cut off. 'Ave been for weeks. Come in on mornin' boat, did you?' She shook her head. 'Long wait till 'e comes back at four, though – less you wanna swim.'

'I hired an inflatable.'

'Did you now? Must be a powerful reason for doin' tha'?'

Kate didn't enlighten her and the woman didn't press the point but, setting the glass in front of her, turned to stab at the illuminated squares on a computer screen on the back wall before re-joining her.

'Where you from then?'

Kate paid her and said, 'Highbridge,' for some reason not yet disclosing the fact that she was a police officer.

''Ighbridge?' the woman echoed, raising painted eyebrows. 'Bloody dump, tha' place. Wha' you doin' 'ere then?'

The moment of truth.

Inwardly wincing and anticipating the change in attitude, Kate produced her warrant card. 'Police,' she said. 'Detective Sergeant Kate Lewis.'

The attitude change was immediate. 'Peroxide' straightened from her leaning position on the bar, her eyes narrowing appreciably. 'P'lice, is it?' she said. 'A woman too, eh – and a sergeant?'

Kate shrugged and smiled again. 'All of that, I'm afraid.'

'Why you 'fraid. Good thing bein' a sergeant *an'* a woman.'

And 'Peroxide' raised her voice as she spoke and stared belligerently around the room, as if challenging a contrary response. But her customers merely grinned back at her, one raising his pint glass in mock salute.

'Exactly,' Kate responded, raising her own glass in a similar fashion. 'A very good thing.'

'Peroxide' rested her elbows on the bar and cupped her hands round her face. 'You 'ere official like?'

Kate took a sip of her cider, suppressed a grimace at its overly sweet taste and produced one of Ellie Landy's photographs. 'Making inquiries into this young woman's death,' she said. 'Ever seen her in here?'

'Peroxide' took the photograph from her, studied it, then slowly shook her head. 'Never seen 'er. She missin' then?'

'Dead,' Kate replied. 'Drowned in the Parrett a few days ago. Thought you'd have read about it in the newspapers.'

'Peroxide' nodded and handed the photograph back. ''Eard about it on local radio but tha's all. Didn't know wha' she looked like. Not seen no paper for days.'

Kate produced a few more photographs and slapped them on the bar. 'Could I leave these with you? One of your customers might have seen her.' She handed over one of her business cards. 'If anyone has any information, they can reach me on this number.'

'Peroxide' nodded and dropped the card into an empty beer glass beside the computer. 'Tha' way, I won't forget,' she said, her false smile broadening. 'Now, another cider, is it?'

Kate shook her head and, draining the glass, set it back on the counter. 'No thanks, but mind if I show the woman's pic around here now?'

'Peroxide' shrugged. 'Please yourself, my duck.'

So Kate did just that. But it was a waste of time. Whether any of the half dozen male customers in the bar had actually seen the girl before, it was impossible to tell, but all shook their heads anyway and returned to their beer, more interested in Kate's figure than anything else and grinning inanely at each other as she went from table to table.

Finally, with a polite nod in the direction of the woman at the bar, Kate headed for the door labelled 'Toilets', ignoring the wolf-whistle that followed her through and smiling briefly to herself in the passageway beyond as she looked for the ladies.

As it turned out, the toilet was clean enough but it smelled strongly of a powerful disinfectant and she couldn't wait to wash her hands and leave again. She didn't get far, however. In the act of pushing through the door back into the bar, she stopped short with one hand frozen against the brass finger plate. A new customer had come into the bar and was standing at the counter talking earnestly to 'Peroxide' – a customer she immediately recognized as her former prisoner, Leroy, the Spliff!

CHAPTER 12

FOR SEVERAL SECONDS Kate just stared at the thin figure. What the hell was the nasty little dealer doing in this particular bar, of all places? And how had he got to the village? Borrowed a boat, like her – or did he own one of his own? Fortunately he had his back towards her and was now concentrating on his newly poured pint, but she knew there was no way she could cross the bar to the entrance doors without running the risk of being spotted by him if he happened to turn his head at the wrong moment.

She was still trying to make up her mind what to do next when the situation took an even worse turn. Responding to a waved glass, the barmaid wiggled to the other end of the counter to serve the impatient customer and, as she did so, Kate saw Leroy idly pick up one of the photos she had left on the counter to give it the once-over. Almost immediately he stiffened, then beckoned 'Peroxide' back to him as she finished serving the other customer. For a few moments he engaged her in an intense conversation, which ended with the woman shrugging and waving a hand towards the door to the toilets. The implication was plain, and as Leroy jerked round to look her way, Kate allowed the door to close gently against her and stood there for a moment, her heart thudding heavily.

Damn it! The vicious little dealer was the last person she'd expected to run into in this godforsaken spot and she felt a stab of apprehension at the thought of what he might do if he managed to get hold of her. Alone, with the only possibility of backup miles away on the other side of acres of flooded fields, she was acutely conscious of her vulnerability. OK, so she could stay in the bar where there were other people but she couldn't remain there for ever and she had no idea how reliable the staff or their clientele were anyway. For all she knew, they could all be inbreds, who would relish the prospect of seeing a police officer getting her comeuppance.

Acutely conscious of the fact that Leroy might already be making his way towards her, she shrank back from the door, glancing quickly around her. Apart from the doors to the male and female toilets, there was a door at the end of the short passageway with a big 'Exit' sign above it and she lunged towards it, grabbing the handle and bursting through into a small square yard with a pair of open gates to her right.

Beyond the gates was an empty car park – hardly surprising it was empty, since the village had become an island with the only road in under at least six feet of water. Following the wall of the public house along to the end, she found herself at the front of the building – at which point she froze again. Far from coming to look for her, Leroy was actually on his way out of the bar again, turning up the collar of his coat against the driving rain.

Surprised, but very relieved, Kate considered her options. She could return to the relative security of the bar, or she could seize her chance and make for her borrowed boat; at least then she would be out of harm's way. But neither option appealed to her. She was bothered by Leroy's reaction to the information he must have gleaned from 'Peroxide' that she was in the village. She would have expected him to have made an effort to find her, to exact some sort of thuggish revenge, but instead, he had simply left the place – almost as if the fact that she was there had spooked him. But why?

And where was he off to in such a rush?

Curiosity winning the day, she stepped out into the rain-soaked street and went after him, keeping her distance and moving only very slowly in case he happened to glance behind him, yet keeping his distinctive figure in view the whole time.

Leroy was obviously a man on a mission and someone who knew exactly where he was going, and he looked neither left nor right, but ploughed into the rain with quick urgent steps, his shoulders hunched into his short coat and his hands thrust deep into the pockets.

A couple of hundred yards from the pub, he turned into another narrow street, flanked by a row of terraced cottages on one side and a high stone wall on the other. Shortly afterwards the wall made a right-angled turn across the street, effectively sealing it off as a cul-de-sac, and Kate spotted a tall wooden gate directly ahead.

Leroy didn't hesitate but, briefly pausing by the gate, he reached upwards and tugged on something – presumably a bell of some sort. A brief conversation evidently followed, though Kate could not make anything out, except a growling sound from a hidden speaker and Leroy's characteristic 'Yo,' before the gate – apparently electronically controlled – slid back to admit him. Then he vanished inside and the gate started to close.

Instinctively, Kate went for it at a run, the edge of the heavy frame clipping her shoulder as she dived through the opening.

Beyond, a neatly manicured driveway snaked through six-foot high shrubs to a big, two-storey Victorian-style house, with a single square tower at one end. Bright lights showed in virtually all the windows and the tower radiated a dimmer more ghostly glow through what appeared to be narrow elongated apertures, like those of a castle keep. The architecture of the building reminded Kate of a folly she had once seen in the grounds of a National Trust property, but, unlike the latter, this place had about as much welcoming warmth as a mausoleum.

Leroy was only yards ahead of her now and, fearful of being spotted by the dealer should he happen to look round, she ducked into the shrubbery to her left to give him time to put a little more distance between them. As it transpired, however, she allowed him too much time, for when she finally stepped back out on to the driveway, he had disappeared.

For a moment she stood there, staring at the house through the gaps in the shrubbery and listening intently. The only sound was the rain drumming on the driveway and rattling on the broad leaves of the bordering shrubs.

Now what? She was in but in where? What was this place and why had Leroy made a beeline for it after learning of her arrival in the village? Could this be where Horse's 'Mr Big' was holed up? Her stomach was beginning to churn again and she tapped her thigh to make sure her police radio was still there. Her fingers touched a flimsy harness, but nothing else. The radio was not in it anymore. As acid spurted into her stomach like molten lava, she suddenly remembered that she had inadvertently left the set in the car when she and Hayden had been carrying out their house-to-house inquiries. She hadn't thought about the thing at the time, because she hadn't needed to use it – even the control room call had been made to Hayden instead of to her, otherwise she would have been alerted to her lapse when the call had come through. 'You stupid bitch,' she breathed. 'You'll forget your bloody head next!' Now she was cut off completely. Her colleagues couldn't even pinpoint her location by using the digital tracking device that was built into all the force's sophisticated TETRA radios, or if they did, the signal would home in on wherever the CID car happened to be at any given moment – more than likely the car park at the nick or her home address in Burtle where Hayden had gone to wolf down a sandwich!

What a prize cock-up!

Common sense dictated that she beat a hasty retreat, returned to the dinghy; quit the village and called for backup from the first available phone. She just hoped the inflatable was still there, because it had suddenly dawned on her that, as well as leaving her phone in the car, she had stupidly left the key in the boat's ignition, which meant that, if some wandering 'tea leaf' happened on to the thing, it might not be there by the time she got back anyway.

And even more fundamental to the issue was one glaringly obvious fact – she had got into the grounds of the house all right, but how the hell was she going to get out again? The exit gate was electronically controlled and the wall enclosing the property had to be at least nine feet high with what looked like gleaming strands of barbed wire along the top. Coupled with which, if by some miracle she did manage to get safely back to the inflatable, exactly what would she be requesting backup for? So far all she had established was the fact that a known drugs dealer had made a visit to a big Victorian house; no crime there and Roscoe would do his crust if this turned out to be yet another red herring that impacted on the NCA operation.

No, all she could do for the present was have a look around; see if she could find anything that would warrant calling in the heavy mob – provided she could get out of the place again to make the call afterwards, of course.

To approach the house on a direct route was not a good idea – though she could see no sign of surveillance cameras, she had no idea who might be looking out of the windows – so instead she ducked back into the shrubbery and made her way through it to one side of the old building. Then, emerging from cover in a darker area, she crossed a section of hard-standing and hugged the side of the building until she reached an enclosed yard at the rear, accessed via a wide ungated archway, set in a high stone wall.

Overall the yard was pretty unremarkable – just a large flagged area, flanked on one side by the house and on the other by two slate-roofed barns equipped with tightly pad-locked double doors. But her curiosity was aroused by the presence of two large lorries, parked close together, facing towards the archway. They appeared to be horseboxes, but climbing on to a rear wheel of each and shining her torch through a side window, she found that they were both completely empty.

She frowned, cupping her hands over her face to wipe off the rain. One horsebox would have been quite normal, but two did seem a bit weird – especially as there was no sign of a stable in the yard nor any sight, sound or smell of horses. Re-checking the barns, she found that, though closed and padlocked, the doors did not quite meet in the middle. Shining her torch through the narrow gap in each, she saw only a stack of large wooden crates and certainly no horses or the customary wooden stalls.

Kate was now totally mystified. True, the animals could have been in a field before the floods and then moved to somewhere more secure afterwards, as was the case with a large proportion of the Levels livestock, but those big empty wagons looked somehow incongruous in the bare walled yard and she couldn't help wondering what possible purpose they served.

Moving closer to the rear of the house, she checked a small recessed door, but found it was locked and the windows flanking it heavily curtained, so it was impossible to see into the room. It was the same story a few yards further on – a locked door and curtained windows that didn't even betray a chink of light. Someone obviously valued their privacy a great deal.

But then, maybe ten to fifteen yards from an archway set in the corresponding perimeter wall at the far end of the yard, she noticed a ghostly light spilling out on to the paving stones. It seemed to be coming from somewhere low down and, peering through the rain, she glimpsed an iron railing enclosing a faintly glowing rectangle, close to the house wall. A basement of some sort, she guessed.

A few strides and she was leaning over the railing, peering down into a narrow enclosure, accessed by a flight of stone steps. There was another door and beside it, a window, curtained like the others, but issuing a wide swathe of light where the curtains had only been partially pulled across.

Intensely curious, she took a chance and followed the steps down, then stared in astonishment through the gap. The room inside was about thirty feet square and kitted out as some kind of laboratory. There were three long benches, two with integral basins and stubby taps and carrying a variety of glass test tubes, retorts and bulbous jars, some linked by rubber tubing. The third bench incorporated three electric hotplates and an array of bottles and shallow pans. A six to seven foot high section of shelving against the far wall was stacked with tins, bottles and plastic containers and alongside this were positioned two enormous American style refrigerators, their indicator lights glowing fiercely like tiny green eyes. The whole place was lit by high level strip-lights and in two corners big ugly ventilation tubes protruded from the ceiling.

Kate had seen something similar to this – though on a very much smaller scale – during her time attached to the drug squad in Bristol and she suspected that what she was looking at was a very sophisticated laboratory for the manufacture of illegal narcotics.

The lab appeared to be empty now, which meant that either the 'cooks' had flown or they had taken a break from their labours. Either way, she needed to get into the place to confirm her suspicions. Risky, but essential.

Holding her breath, she tried the small door – only to find it was securely locked. Damn it! She had to find another way inside the house or all her efforts would have been for nothing.

Climbing back up the steps to the yard, she moved on and this time got lucky. There was a frosted sash-type window some thirty feet beyond the basement area, just before the second archway, which had been left partially open at the bottom. Even before she ducked down to peer through the gap, the distinctive raw smell emanating from inside told her that she was about to break into the house via a downstairs toilet. Ah well, *c'est la vie*.

Checking that the place was empty, she heaved gently under the lower part of the window frame with both hands and was able to raise it a couple of feet, wincing at its squeal of protest. Then, clambering up on to the low sill, she grabbed hold of the frame again, to swing one leg over the sill and squeeze through the gap.

Fortunately, the toilet seat was down, which at least provided a firm footing for her as she hauled herself inside, but it was a tight squeeze and she felt her anorak rip on the window catch before she managed to touch the floor.

Silence but for the sound of a washbasin tap spurting and gurgling loudly. Irritated by the sound, she reached over and turned the tap off. The window then began to rattle in a draught and she reached behind her to close it completely before moving slowly towards the door.

The door opened with just a faint creak and light flooded into the room. She peered round the frame in both directions. To her right was a blank wall, but to her left a long thickly carpeted corridor led away from her. A couple of gilt embellished white doors opened off on both sides of the passage and big terracotta pots, boasting three-foot high exotic plants, stood between each of them, a wooden staircase thrusting its way into view just beyond. The corridor itself was deserted.

Her feet made hardly any sound in the thick pile of the

carpet and, ignoring the closed doors on either side, she made straight for the staircase, pausing at the bottom and looking around her for the stairs leading down to the basement. She found them after backtracking a few feet, hidden behind a curtain drawn across what at first sight appeared to be an alcove of some sort. Unlike the main staircase, which was thickly carpeted like the corridor and seemed to be constructed of solid oak, the basement stairs were made of plain wrought iron and even from where she was standing, she could detect the strong smell of chemicals rising from below.

The stairs rattled as she began the descent and she felt the whole structure shaking under her, as if the nuts and bolts that held it together were straining against themselves and gradually loosening. She was only too pleased to reach the bottom and relieved that she had met no one else coming up, but now, in the dimly lit basement corridor, she felt a sense of impending calamity and almost turned round and ran back up the stairs again.

Resisting the urge, she moved on, passing a couple of built-in cupboards on her left, the first of which she found to contain a massive water tank, fitted with an immersion heater and a tangle of electrical wires and pipes and the second, an ancient stone-cold boiler which filled the entire space. A third and final door on her right, just before the corridor ended in a solid brick wall, turned out to access the laboratory. She was surprised to find it unlocked – but there again, why would anyone worry about security when access to the house was controlled by an electrically operated gate and the grounds enclosed by a nine-foot high wall, surmounted by barbed wire?

An even stronger chemical smell rushed out to greet her as she opened the door and she pulled out a handkerchief to cover the lower part of her face before stepping inside. The fumes were lethal, despite the inbuilt ventilation system, but she had no intention of staying longer than necessary anyway and satisfied herself relatively quickly by checking some of the tins, bottles and plastic containers on the shelves she had noted earlier.

Most of them had innocent labels, suggesting the contents to be mundane products, such as sports drinks, apple juice and Pepsi Cola, but others were labelled more blatantly. Several crudely written labels jumped out at her – sodium bicarbonate, acetic anhydride, iodine, ether, anhydrous ammonia, ephedrine and pseudoephedrine – chemicals she remembered from her Bristol drug squad days as being used as precursors in the manufacture of such illicit narcotics as methamphetamine, cocaine, heroin and morphine.

She emitted a low involuntary whistle, appreciating the importance of her discovery. This was not some amateur backstreet drugs kitchen, but a state-of-the-art laboratory – manufacturing not just one kind of narcotic but a whole multitude of them – which suggested the involvement of a team of experienced professional chemists. It was like some kind of obscene criminal supermarket, supplying whatever the illicit market demanded, with dealer clients certain to be not only in Somerset, but throughout the UK and beyond.

She knew from past experience that many of the criminal gangs involved in drugs trafficking had now moved out of the cities into the rural areas because of the heat generated by the police and enforcement agencies, and this underworld enterprise was a classic example of this new trend, if it could be called that.

No wonder Ellie Landy and poor little Polly had been eliminated.

Ellie had obviously stumbled upon the activities of the syndicate through Polly and both had paid for the disclosures with their lives. Proving the link between the cartel and the murders would not be easy, but the lab was a very good start. All Kate had to do was to alert the police control room to what she had discovered, but in her present circumstances, trapped inside this big rambling property in a marooned village, with no means of communication with the outside world, 'all' was a very big word.

CHAPTER 13

DI Roscoe got the telephone call mid-afternoon and he stiffened in his chair when he found out who the caller was, as if sensing that more bad news was on the way.

'Lydia Summers,' the forensic pathologist announced cheerfully. 'Got some interesting info for you about the Ellie Landy case.'

Roscoe grunted. 'Like what?' he replied warily.

There was a heavy sigh on the other end of the phone. 'You don't have to sound so enthusiastic,' Summers said.

Roscoe pushed his gum to the side of his mouth. 'Get on with it, Doc,' he said. 'I'm busy.'

Another sigh. 'Aren't we all, Ted. Well, the fact is, I sent samples from the scene of the incident to specialist forensic botanists – a lichenologist and a limnologist – and we have just had preliminary reports back, which make interesting reading. I'm about to send you copies over by email, but I expect to receive the full definitive reports in the next few days.'

'And what's a lichen ... whatever, and the other thing, when it's at home?'

She laughed. 'Lichenologists study lichen and fungi; Limnologists, aquatic organisms.'

Roscoe snorted. 'Something else I've learned then,' he said drily. 'So, in a nutshell...?'

Summers took the hint. 'Tests on the material found in the

torn fingernails have revealed the presence of a new form of a rare Lecanactis or Churchyard lichen—'

'So?'

'I'm not a lichenologist, but I understand that this particular organism is only found in churchyard environments, which would suggest that the deceased's hand came in contact with an affected surface at some stage.'

'So you're saying Landy died in a churchyard?'

'No, what I am saying is that her fingers must have scraped along a stone surface bearing traces of this lichen. Apparently, it is usually found on the external north or east facing walls of churchyards and it is sensitive to rain and light. This particular lichen is not found in rivers, so Ellie Landy would not have picked it up from the Parrett.'

'A graveyard then?'

'Not necessarily – it could be the wall of a church or on a tomb, something like that – and the interesting thing is that an examination of the lichen's condition has indicated that it probably suffered from a severe degenerative change in its environment – too much sun.'

Roscoe snorted derisively. 'Not much of that around here lately.'

She laughed. 'Or too much water – which seems more likely after what the Levels have been subjected to lately.' She was serious again. 'The important thing is that all this suggests the deceased was alive and struggling when her hand scraped along an affected surface and that, since the lichen present under her fingernails is more or less unique to churchyards, it suggests that Ellie Landy did not die in the River Parrett but was actually dead before she entered the river.'

'So how did she end up in the Parrett?'

'That's for you to determine. I only present you with my professional conclusions, based on the forensic evidence obtained – and there is more. A substantial quantity of fluid found in the deceased's lungs contained a small quantity of diatoms—'

'Dia- what? You've lost me, Doc.'

'Diatoms are eukaryotic algae and populate both fresh and sea water in vast numbers and there are said to be thousands of different species. It is possible to link a deceased person to the place of their demise by comparing the particular species of diatom found, say in a river, to the species found in the corpse.

'When a person drowns, they absorb diatoms with the water and these eventually permeate the tissues and organs of the deceased – the lungs, the brain, the kidneys, the liver etcetera, but this can only happen while the person is alive and the respiratory system is still operating; a bit like a suction pump. Once they are deceased, the diatoms cannot be absorbed. If Ellie Landy had died in the River Parrett, one would have expected to find large numbers of diatoms in her system of the same species as those present in the river. Instead, our forensic limnologists discovered an entirely different species in her body which was not present in a controlled sample taken from the river.'

Roscoe took a deep breath. 'Can't say I understand your point entirely, Doc, but in essence, you're still maintaining Landy's death was suspicious then?'

'Exactly, Ted,' Summers said, her voice now more brittle. 'I believe she was unlawfully killed in one place and dumped in the river afterwards to make the incident look like an acci-dental drowning.'

Roscoe was fumbling for his cigarettes now, still confused. 'So we do have a murder on our hands then?' he growled.

'How you actually categorize it in the end is a matter for you, Ted,' she retorted. 'However, based on the forensic evi-dence I have put before you, I'd suggest that the coroner would expect your department to have a radical re-think on the cause of Ellie Landy's death, but I'll leave that decision to you.'

Roscoe returned the telephone to its cradle. 'Bloody Nora!' he said aloud and quickly dialled the DCI's number.

Kate spotted the internal door just as she was about to leave the laboratory and, like the main door to the lab, someone had carelessly left it unlocked.

Trying the handle, she found that the door opened easily and lights sprang on automatically inside. The room beyond turned out to be a storeroom, about seven foot square and completely windowless. The whole of one side was occupied by cardboard boxes, stacked one on top of the other and carrying innocuous labels, such as GKR Health Foods, Stampers flour and Newbold Medicinal Products. A quick check on the contents of a couple of them revealed, firstly, tightly packed plastic bottles, containing circular white tablets, not unlike those sold as vitamins by companies dispensing medicinal supplements, and, secondly, large transparent bags of white powder, individually labelled as 'Bread flour' and about the same size as those sold in supermarkets. She was quite sure anyone checking the top layers of the boxes would find either vitamin supplements or bread flour too, but underneath it was bound to be a totally different story. Now she realized what those big crates in the two barns contained – probably enough illegal substances to feed every addict in a city the size of London or New York for a year or more! The scale of the thing was mind-blowing.

She had no idea as to the exact nature of the narcotics the different boxes she was checking contained and, unlike the police detectives in some of the more outlandish fictional film dramas, she had no intention of sampling any of them to find out, as it would invariably have meant her going on a trip herself. Instead, she satisfied herself by delving first into one of the boxes of tablets and slipping a plastic bottle from the second or third row down into her pocket for subsequent analysis and using another of the bottles to collect a sample from one of the bags of white powder now at the bottom of the box, after first emptying the tablets into her other pocket.

Anxious not to outstay her welcome, she then quietly left the storeroom and slipped out of the laboratory, back into the corridor. And it was at this point that she heard voices above her head and the sound of footsteps ringing on the iron stairs she was about to climb.

Whirling round in a panic, she looked for somewhere to hide. There was nowhere. Behind her was just another blank wall and in front of her, just the two cupboards she had passed on her way to the laboratory.

A foot and trouser leg appeared below the line of the corridor ceiling, followed by the hem of a white coat. Then someone laughed and as the other foot joined the first, the man in question stopped, turning slightly, apparently to speak to someone coming down behind him. At the same moment Kate spotted the gap under the stairs and virtually threw herself at it, scrambling into the open space seconds before the white coat moved off again and stepped down into the corridor.

Crouched under the wrought iron steps, Kate felt about as exposed as it was possible to feel. The latticework construction of the individual treads meant that it was possible for anyone above to see straight through them and all those on the stairs had to do was to look down and she was done for. But, even as she waited with baited breath for the shout that meant discovery, nothing happened and the white coats – she could see through the stairs that there were at least three of them – reached the corridor and went straight into the laboratory. The chemists were back at work.

The stairs seemed to be deliberately trying to attract attention as she made her way back to the upper floor, but she resisted the impulse to move more quickly; it would only have made things worse. But it was stressful trying to hold herself back and she was sure that one of the white coats would reappear at any moment to check on the noise she was making.

Either they were hard of hearing or they had the lab door closed, however, and she gained the upper level without being challenged.

Then, carefully pulling back one side of the curtain masking the stairs and checking both ways to make sure the ground floor corridor was clear, she stepped out into the open and turned right, intending to head back to the toilet via which she had gained entry to the house in the first place. She had only managed a couple of yards, however, when she heard a door slam from somewhere behind her and, instinctively shrinking behind one of the big potted plants, she glimpsed a black-suited man coming towards her along the corridor.

There was a door just feet away from her and she inched her way along the wall towards it. She had no idea whether or not the door was locked or what or who might be on the other side, but with the approaching man just seconds away, she was fresh out of options.

She found the door handle and turned it. At first it remained firm, but then the door suddenly gave way and she stumbled backwards into the room, nudging the door to with the toe of her boot as the black suit strode past the plant pot. Peering after him through the gap between the door and the frame, she saw him open a second door a few feet further on and disappear inside the room, slamming the door after him.

Releasing a long tremulous sigh of relief, Kate stared around her. She was in an ornate bathroom with a huge kidney-shaped bath, gold-plated taps and a corner jacuzzi. The window was heavily curtained and subdued light emanated from a large ceiling globe. Another gilt-embellished white door provided a connection to the room beyond, which Kate guessed might be a bedroom or some sort of study – probably exhibiting the same kind of opulence. So much for the adage that crime didn't pay!

She was almost tempted to check to see what was on the

other side of that door, her curiosity almost overcoming her common sense, but then she thought better of it and it was a good job that she did. The man's voice seemed so close that she whirled round in a panic – for a moment thinking he was standing behind her, then realizing to her relief that he was actually in the next room – and speaking to someone else.

'Where did you put our little fat man?' The voice was soft, cultured and strangely menacing in the way the question was put. Kate felt a chill run down her spine.

'In the attic room,' another, rougher voice replied.

'Good. That will teach him to come snooping around my private premises. Who is he?'

'Guy called Gabriel Lessing. Says he's from a news agency.'

There was a loud hiss, a bit like the sharp spit from fat spilling on to a hot stove. 'A journalist? That could be bad for us. What does he know?'

'Dunno yet,' the rough voice replied.

'So find out! I want to know who he is, how he knew about this place and who he has told – and I want to know like yesterday.'

'He won't say anything.'

Another, longer hiss. 'Then we shall have to use some *persuasion*, won't we? But first, wheel Leroy in.'

Kate's mind was in turmoil. Gabriel Lessing? Shit! How the hell had the disreputable agency man got himself into such a desperate situation? Whatever the answer, he was now obviously being held captive and about to be subjected to some form of cruel torture to make him talk. It was incredibly horrible and didn't bear thinking about. She had to do something and quickly, but what? She had no idea where the attic room was, except that it had to be at the top of the house – and what did she expect to achieve on her own anyway? She had never needed backup more than she needed it at this precise moment, but with her police radio probably now lying somewhere on the floor of the CID car and her own personal mobile still at home, she had no means of contacting anyone and she had about as much chance of getting hold of a phone as getting out of the grounds of this damned house without being spotted. As she pondered the impossibility of her own situation, she was distracted by another chilling development.

'We got a problem, Boss,' Leroy's distinctive voice blurted a second after a door had closed with a bang and Kate sensed a nervous tremor in the drug pusher's tone.

'What sort of a problem?' the other man said almost wearily.

'It's some *POL*-ice chick—'

'Police? What are you on about?'

'Some pig 'tec been pokin' her nose in fings. Done nicked me on sus—'

'Yes, I know all about that. You've been careless, it seems, but we'll come to that in a minute.'

'No worries, Boss. The fuzz ain't got noffink on me. They chucked me out again anyway, but this 'tec, she here now – in Lowmoor.'

'What? How do you know?'

'She been to the pub snoopin' around and showin' that dead press chick's pic there. Mavis in bar tol' me.'

Another sharp hiss. 'And you came straight to me after leaving the pub? You imbecile! That detective could have seen you and followed you here!'

There was a choking noise as saliva seemed to collect in Leroy's throat and his reply cut through it in a bubbling response. 'No chance Boss. I real careful. She don't see me. Honest.'

'You've become a liability, Leroy,' the words came to Kate softly, but with even heavier menace, 'and I don't like liabilities, you know that. I brought you into the syndicate to be my front man, but you have been a big disappointment to me. You had the right credentials and some very good contacts, so at the beginning I foolishly believed you would be an asset to me. All you had to do was use your contacts to market my products to the right people through the Sapphire Club and I paid you well but it wasn't enough for you, was it? You wanted more.'

'No, Boss, I cool, I swear.'

There was a brittle laugh. 'Cool, are you, Leroy? Is that why you've been doing some dealing on your own account, eh – because you're cool? Stealing my stuff and selling it on? Did you think I wouldn't find out about that junkie, Polly, and the fact that you wasted her in case she said too much to the wrong people?'

Leroy's voice had died to a whine now and Kate could almost picture him on his knees before the other man. 'No, Boss, I ain't done no dealin'. I just—'

'Lies, Leroy, they spill off your tongue like spittle, and this operation is too big to be compromised by a little shit like you.'

There was a scuffling sound, then a sharp cry, which was abruptly cut off in a choking gasping sound which seemed to go on for ever. Then the man Leroy had referred to as 'Boss' spoke again.

'Get rid of the body, Tommy,' he said. 'I don't want him found – ever.'

'Good as done,' the rough voice replied. 'Sorry about the claret on the carpet.'

Another brittle laugh. 'Forget it. I fancy you were just a bit too enthusiastic with your garrotte! But, more importantly, once you've got rid of him, sort out our guest upstairs, eh? I want answers, whatever it takes.'

'You got it, Mr Pavlović.'

'And get a couple of the boys to search the grounds. In the absence of the CCTV cameras I realize I should have had installed, we shall have to do a physical search. Just make sure we haven't got any other unwelcome visitors, eh?'

'Like the woman cop?'

'You catch on fast, Tommy, you could end up on *Mastermind* one day!'

In the next room, Kate swayed drunkenly, her senses reeling. She had just been privy to a brutal murder. It was obvious that Leroy had been dispatched as callously as an abattoir animal. For a few moments she desperately tried to control the violent spasms of reflux that were the inevitable consequence of her horrific realization and she held on to the nearby sink tightly to stop her legs from folding under her.

Leroy had not amounted to much – a complete waste of a skin, in fact – but he had been a human being and he had just been murdered just feet away from where she was standing. So, what the hell did she do about it? And, more importantly, what *could* she do about it? Marching into the next room and shouting, 'Police, you're under arrest,' was hardly a feasible move. So what was the most sensible thing to do? Get out of the house and back to her boat ASAP obviously, but what about Gabriel Lessing? She could hardly leave him to the horrific fate that had been reserved for him. No, somehow she had to find the attic room while Tommy was disposing of Leroy's corpse, and then try and get them both away from the place before Lessing's disappearance was discovered.

She heard a dragging sound from the next room and a series of heavy grunts. Then a door opened and closed with a bang. Tommy was on his way with Leroy's body.

Kate crept to the bathroom door and listened. There wasn't a sound outside. Nevertheless, remembering the thickness of the corridor carpet and its capacity to mask footfalls, she held herself in check and opened the door just a crack. Peering around the frame, she satisfied herself that the corridor to her left was empty and that Tommy had gone. She thrust her head out further and checked the right-hand section. Nothing, just a long empty corridor. She took a deep breath and stepped out, hesitated and threw a rueful glance in the direction of the toilet which could have provided her with a rapid escape route, before turning right, back towards the stairs – and heaven alone knew what.

CHAPTER 14

TED ROSCOE WAS very uneasy. After his telephone confab with the pathologist, Ellie Landy's so-called 'accidental death' didn't look quite as much of an accident as it had before. Even the DCI had looked to be wavering when Roscoe'd passed the latest forensic information on to him, the tic in his left cheek giving the game away as he'd smoothed his blond moustache with the finger and thumb of one hand, while his sharp blue eyes darted quick nervous glances at the DI across the desk. Not that he'd shown any immediate sign of backtracking on his earlier decision, however.

It was all right playing bloody politics, Roscoe mused after returning to his office – keeping things nailed down to avoid launching another major crime inquiry, with all the unpopular resource implications involved – but he was long enough in the tooth to know that, if things went pear-shaped, DCI Toby Ricketts would conveniently forget his previous insistence on a low-key inquiry and do the quickest about-turn imaginable. That meant one Ted Roscoe would end up carrying a very hot can as the senior case officer, while Ricketts absolved himself of all responsibility, claiming he had been given insufficient information on which to base his earlier judgment.

Outwardly, Roscoe was very loyal to his boss and, being an ex-military man, he tended towards obedience to orders, even if he didn't necessarily agree with what he was being told to do. But that didn't mean he had to respect the person who was giving the orders. He was one truculent, down-to-earth old-stager who had an inherent distrust of the new brand of senior rank, especially those recruited under the fast-track system, straight from university, like the blond good-looking Detective Chief Inspector Toby Ricketts, for instance. Brought up with rough, hard-drinking 'guv'nors', like himself – the real-life versions of such fictional TV hard men as seventies Detective Chief Superintendent Charlie Barlow in *Softly, Softly: Taskforce* and Detective Inspector Jack Regan in *The Sweeney*. Roscoe had little time for the new educated 'wuzzits', as he called them, with their baby-faces, smooth talk and youthful arrogance. A DCI at twenty-eight, he thought savagely? Ricketts was still just a kid. Yeah, but he was also the boss, and that was the problem!

Stuffing a wad of chewing gum in his mouth, Roscoe forgot to remove the silver paper first and spat it out with an oath after the first bite. Throwing it into the wastepaper bin, he produced a battered packet of cigarettes instead and lit up a bent filter-tip, seemingly unaware of the tobacco strands curling out of a tear in the paper.

Where the hell was Kate Lewis? He needed to talk to her before the whatnot hit the fan and she should have been back to the station ages ago. How long did it take to make just a few routine inquiries? He was on the point of ringing the control room to call her up on her radio, when a knock on the office door preceded the looming bulk of Hayden Lewis.

'Sorry, sir,' Hayden exclaimed, 'but I'm worried about Kate.'

The DC's face was very red and his eyes had the sharp gleam of someone in near mental panic.

Roscoe felt insects crawl around his insides. 'Worried?' he snapped. 'Why?'

Hayden dumped himself in a chair opposite, without invitation, and went on in a rush, 'Got called to a burglary in Mark while we were doing some house to house on the Landy job. Had to leave her to it. That was at least two hours ago and I haven't seen or heard from her since.'

'House to house? Why were you doing that? I told her to wrap this inquiry up.'

Hayden looked uncomfortable. 'That's what we were going to do,' he replied after some hesitation, 'but Kate thought we'd make just one or two more inquiries at a hamlet near where the girl's body was found.'

Thinking of what he had learned from the pathologist, together with his own emerging doubts, Roscoe didn't press the point. 'Tried her radio?' he said instead.

Hayden hesitated, looking uncomfortable. 'I found it on the floor of the CID car,' he said lamely. 'She – she obviously left it behind when we were doing our house to house and forgot about it afterwards.'

Roscoe looked as though he was going to explode. 'She did *what?*' he rasped. 'An experienced DS leaves her personal radio *in the car*? What sort of DS is she?'

Hayden winced, then gave a heavy sigh. 'These things happen, sir,' he said, keen to move on. 'But the thing is, we now have no means now of contacting her to make sure she's OK.'

Roscoe glared at him for a moment then shook his head in disbelief before stubbing out his cigarette and reaching for some more gum. 'Exactly where did you leave her?'

'By some cottages – maybe half a mile from the village of Lowmoor. Said she wanted to finish checking them out before packing the job in. That should only have taken her another twenty minutes or so at the most.'

'What about Lowmoor? She could have decided to extend her inquiries there?'

'If she did, she'd have needed to be a good swimmer. Place is cut off by the floods.'

Roscoe stared at him in mid-chew, gum wedged between his front teeth like a large wad of white Plasticine. 'And she's been out of contact for two hours?'

Hayden glanced at his watch. 'Nearer three actually. My burglary job tied me up for longer than I'd anticipated and I didn't get away from Mark until an hour ago.'

Roscoe chewed rapidly again, at first saying nothing. Then he barked, 'OK, better get some initial inquiries carried out. Might be nothing in it – the silly cow is a bloody maverick and she's has done this sort of Lone Ranger thing before, so we don't want to hit the panic button too soon.'

Hayden scowled at him, plainly not appreciating his offensive description of his wife. 'And what if she's in trouble – fallen in the water somewhere or been hit on by some pervert?'

Roscoe met his gaze levelly. 'Hardly likely, is it? Your missus may be a bit of a loose cannon at times, but she's a pretty tough cookie.'

'Perhaps we could get the chopper up anyway?'

The agony of indecision was etched in Roscoe's expression and he blew a bubble with his gum, sucking it back in under his moustache almost immediately. 'We could, but if this turns out to be a false alarm, we'd look bloody stupid – and Kate certainly wouldn't thank us for it.'

Hayden's mouth tightened and his blue eyes flashed angrily. 'So we just sit tight and do nothing then – is that what you're saying?'

Roscoe's slab-like face hardened. 'No,' he rasped, 'that *isn't* what I'm saying. You grab a couple of uniforms and get out to where you left her pronto; maybe someone in one of the cottages will know where she went. If we draw a blank there, *then* I'll think about sending the balloon up. Satisfied?'

'No,' Hayden retorted. 'I'm not.'

Roscoe glared at him. 'Tough!' he said. 'She should have hung on to her radio then, shouldn't she?'

The staircase was wide and heavily carpeted. Kate's leather boots made little sound as she headed for the upper floor, acutely conscious of the fact that, if anyone happened to come down at the same time, she had nowhere to hide. She had no idea where the killer, Tommy, had gone; hopefully he was still fully occupied dumping Leroy's body somewhere outside, which meant he was unlikely to be making for the attic yet to interrogate Gabriel Lessing. But she knew she still had very little time at her disposal. She had to find the room, somehow gain access, as the door would almost certainly be locked, and get away with Lessing before Tommy reappeared. And even then, the pair of them would still have to get out of the grounds of the house and away from what had become an island with possibly an army of thugs in pursuit. No mean task!

Her heartbeat had become a hammer against her chest when she reached the top of the staircase and checked the top-floor corridor in both directions. Nothing, save the same ubiquitous white doors with their gilt embellishments and a thick carpet. So where was the access staircase to the attic? Then she remembered her first sight of the house and the tower at one end. That had to be where the attic room was located.

Closing her eyes tightly for a second, she tried to visualize the front of the building as she had first seen it. The tower had been on the right and, as far as she could work out with the curve of the staircase, she was now facing the front, which meant the tower was to her left. Taking a deep trembling breath, she turned in that direction – and seconds later spotted the deep recess on her right, with a narrow staircase ascending to another floor. She breathed a sigh of relief.

The staircase reminded her of one she had once climbed to a church bell tower as a child, though this tower was nowhere near as high, and there was a light switch at the bottom. Nevertheless, as with the church bell tower, it curled round and round like a corkscrew until she reached a stout wooden door. She tried the handle. The door was locked and no key was in evidence. She swore under her breath. Now what?

She was actually on the point of admitting defeat and retracing her steps when, quite by chance, her hand scraped the left hand wall and something jangled. Glancing down, she saw a black mortice-type key swinging gently on a hook close to the door frame. Eureka! Obviously the Sandman and his crew hadn't envisaged someone having the nerve to break into the house and had chosen convenience over security where access to the tower room was concerned. Well, they were in for a shock!

Unhooking the key, she carefully inserted it in the lock, breathed a quick prayer, and turned it to the right. The lock snapped open and, turning the ring handle, she lifted an iron latch and the door swung inwards on well-oiled hinges.

The room beyond was only about seven foot square, lit by a three stem chandelier, and it contained an assortment of furniture, boxes and rolls of carpet. It had obviously been used as a storeroom at one time – what Kate's Irish mum would have called a 'bogey hole' – but it was serving a much more sinister purpose now.

Gabriel Lessing was sitting on a wooden crate in one corner, his hands tied behind him and, as it turned out, then secured to a metal pipe attached to the wall, and his ankles lashed together. He was wearing just a shirt, which was badly soiled and ripped in one place, and grey corduroy trousers. The khaki coat he had been wearing when Kate had last seen him by the River Parrett was lying on the floor at his feet with a pair of gumboots dumped on top of it.

His face was puffed and bloodied and there was a look of terrified expectancy in his brown eyes when she first appeared. But it quickly began to fade when he saw who his visitor was.

'I – I've been kidnapped and beaten,' he said unnecessarily. 'I – I demand police protection.'

She smiled grimly at his farcical comments and dug one

hand into her pocket, producing the small clasp knife she always carried and pulling out one of the sharp blades.

'Keep still,' she ordered as she leaned over him to begin cutting the thick cords off his wrists. 'What the hell were you doing here?'

'Just taking pictures of the gates and wall. Then this big thug grabbed me from behind and hauled me inside.'

Kate paused in the middle of cutting through the cords, her curiosity aroused in spite of their predicament. 'You knew about this place all along, didn't you?' she accused. 'Did Ellie Landy tell you about it before she died? You've been lying to us, haven't you?'

Lessing swallowed hard, his eyes darting from side to side like a trapped animal. 'She – she only said she was chasing a big story. I didn't know what.'

'And what else? You'd better tell me or I'll leave you here.'

'She – she just said it was some sort of criminal conspiracy centred on a big house in – in a hilltop village cut off by the floods. I got hold of a map and made a few in–inquiries....'

She finished cutting through the cords binding his wrists and turned her attention to those around his ankles. 'And put two and two together?' she finished for him. 'So how did you get here?'

He sniffed miserably. 'The morning supply boat.'

She finished cutting through the last of the cords and straightened up.

'Right, get your boots and coat on. We're leaving.'

He grabbed the sleeve of her coat, panic in his eyes. 'They said they would kill me if I made a sound,' he blurted. 'Were – were going to gag me until I told them I was asthmatic—'

'Shut it!' she hissed, cutting him off, and dumped his coat in his lap. 'They'll be on their way up here in a few moments. We have to get out.'

'They took – took my camera and notebook,' he wailed. 'I want them arrested.'

Kate's hand struck him hard across the face. 'I said, shut it, you stupid little turd!' she snarled. 'I don't give a shit about your camera or your notebook. If they find me here, we're *both* dead, got it?'

He was crying now, Kate's none too gentle blow releasing the floodgates of pent-up emotion as if he were a hysterical child, but she felt no sympathy for him, just a sense of revulsion. 'Get your coat and boots on,' she repeated, 'and keep close to me.'

There was no one on the stairs as they left the room and Kate had the foresight to re-lock the door and pocket the key. That would hold up Tommy for a vital few minutes while he tried to find it, she mused.

Surprisingly, they made the corridor and the main staircase to the ground floor without encountering anyone, but then their luck ran out.

Kate heard the voices just as she was about to head along the downstairs corridor towards the toilet through which she had entered the house. Grabbing Lessing by the collar, she took a chance and hauled him through an adjacent door into what turned out to be a broom cupboard as at least two men, talking loudly, strode past.

Giving them a few seconds, she risked a check and saw that the corridor was empty again. 'Come on!' she rapped at Lessing and went to drag him out of the cupboard again. But to her surprise he hesitated, holding back.

'I can't,' he moaned. 'I need my inhaler.'

Kate stared at him incredulously. 'Your inhaler?' she exclaimed in a hoarse whisper. 'You've got to be joking.'

'Can't – can't breathe properly,' he said. 'It's the stress.'

Unceremoniously she jerked him out into the corridor, then pushed him ahead of her. 'Move!' she ordered. 'Or, so help me, I will leave you here!'

He stumbled, but kept going, his breathing now issuing in ragged gasps as she prodded him forward. They reached the toilet without event and, once inside, Kate allowed him the luxury of a very brief rest as she struggled with the window, which seemed to have stuck somehow. His moans and ragged breathing seemed to fill the place and, briefly glancing once over her shoulder, she saw in the fading light filtering in through the window that he was holding on to a towel rail as if his life depended on it.

She could feel her heart making loud squishy noises, like an overworked water pump, as she hauled on the window. It rose a few inches, then jammed again. 'Shit! Shit! Shit!' she snarled, and at the same moment Lessing began to hyper-ventilate behind her and she heard the sound of thudding footsteps above her head accompanied by the faint sound of shouting. Their escape had been discovered. Then the window flew up, nearly taking her hands off.

'Quickly! Outside!' she rapped at Lessing and, heedless of his obvious breathing problems, dragged him to the window. 'Up on the toilet seat and through the window – unless you want to die here now?'

How much of the agency man's condition was down to asthma and how much plain hysteria was unclear, but after some difficulty, he managed to get up on to the seat and over the sill, dropping headfirst on to the hard-standing below the window. Kate was right behind him and she did not allow him any relief, but hauled him to his feet and pushed him towards the archway through which she had entered the yard earlier. As far as she knew, there were no dogs on the premises, so if they could reach the shrubbery at the front of the house, they might be able to lie low there and wait for an opportunity to get out through the electronic gate. It was a long-shot, but it was also their only chance and she felt a sense of hope when she saw and smelled the damp spirals of mist rising from the paving stones; the infamous marsh mist was coming to their aid. But then fickle fate decided to change sides and threw a major obstacle in the way.

That obstacle was what appeared to be a heavily built man whose fuzzy shape appeared in the very archway they were heading for, like a spectral visitant from an alien world.

CHAPTER 15

HAYDEN DIDN'T BOTHER to ask the uniformed shift inspector for two of his officers to assist him with his house to house inquiries, as Roscoe had proposed. He knew without being told that, with government cuts, the uniformed branch was desperately short-staffed and probably only had half-a-dozen bobbies on duty as it was; he had no intention of wasting time making pointless demands for resources that were not available anyway. Instead, he retrieved the keys of the CID car he had been using from the hook beside the door and headed for the police station yard at almost a run.

Twenty minutes and several miles of burned rubber later he slid to a halt in the same gateway he and Kate had used just a few hours before and stumbled out on to the familiar muddy lane. It had stopped raining now, but the flooded fields beyond the lane were fast disappearing in a late afternoon dusk thickened by an emerging white marsh mist, and lights already burned in the windows of most of the cottages. There was no sign of Kate – or anyone else for that matter – and, as he unlatched the gate of the first cottage, he couldn't help wondering whether this was as much a waste of time as it would have been trying for uniformed support. After all, how could any of the local residents possibly know where Kate had gone following her house checks – if, in fact, she had been capable of finishing them in the first place? He frowned as he knocked on the door. Get a grip on things, man, he told himself in an attempt at reassurance, this isn't some awful *Psycho*-type drama! You're over-reacting. Kate's probably got tied up somewhere, nothing more. But that line of thought didn't help him much at all – especially the phrase 'tied up'!

The local residents weren't much use either and he grew increasingly frustrated as his inquiries at cottage after cottage produced nothing but the shake of a head or the shrug of the shoulders. 'She called here, yes,' was the usual response, 'but don't know where she went afterwards.'

Hayden had all but given up when he knocked on the door of the last cottage in the row and he was totally unprepared for the reception he received.

'Borrowed my bloody dinghy,' the thin, sallow-faced young man snapped at him, 'and she ain't returned it yet.'

'Yeah,' the buxom woman said, pushing past him. 'We co-operated with the police and this is what happens.'

Hayden held up both hands to calm them down. 'When was this?' he queried.

The woman frowned. ''Bout three hours ago.'

'But why did she borrow your boat?'

'Tell him, Sam,' the woman encouraged. 'You brought it on yourself, you know, by not reporting things in the first place.'

'Reporting what?'

Sam said nothing, but stared down at his feet. The woman took a deep breath, then said it all for him. 'That girl – the one who drowned? She got Sam to take her across to Lowmoor in his dinghy a couple of days before she was found. The detective sergeant who came here got quite excited when we told her that and leaned on him to lend her the dinghy so she could go there herself.'

'What, to Lowmoor?'

'No, Bristol – what do you think?'

'Yeah,' Sam growled, suddenly activating, 'and that dinghy cost me a bundle. I'll be suing you lot, if she's totalled it.'

But Hayden wasn't interested in his complaint. 'Do you have another boat?'

'Why would I?'

'Anyone else around here have one?'

Sam snorted. 'Why, so you can total theirs as well?'

Hayden's eyes narrowed. 'Just answer the question.'

'No one I know. Local guy been using his inflatable twice a day to ferry people and stuff to and from Lowmoor, but I hear he got engine trouble last trip back, so his boat's laid up for repair in a yard near Burrowbridge.'

Sam smirked, staring past him into the dusk. 'So you'll just have to swim to Lowmoor, won't you?'

Tommy Couchman had been a villain all his life. First, small-time hits as a teenager on other school kids, armed with a flick-knife, then to bigger things, like blaggings on petrol stations and convenience stores, tooled up with a nice shooter. He'd done time, of course – got seven years for one armed robbery, but only because the stupid arse of a bookie had tried to tackle him and got a bullet in his thigh for his trouble.

When he'd come out of stir, though, he'd turned over a new leaf. Blaggings were for dipsticks – there were easier ways of making money and he'd found one of them acting as an enforcer for the syndicate. It was easier because you were preying on your own kind, knocking off or maiming those in the same line of business, and no one was going to worry too much about what happened to other villains, were they? Only thing you had to be sure of was that you were on the winning side, and the syndicate he worked for now – and the Sandman in particular – had no real competitors. That was because they had all been eliminated, just like he had stiffed Leroy. And he grinned as he ran his fingers over the garrotte in his pocket and pushed through the toilet door on the ground floor of the big Victorian house, promising himself that that little turd of a journalist would end up the same way when he found him – and whoever had sprung him from the attic in the first place.

He stared around the toilet and saw the open window immediately. Another grin. He'd guessed as much. He'd known about that dodgy window in the bog for a while; it was important to know everything about your environment if you were to survive. He checked the sill and, with the aid of his torch, saw the scrapes in the paintwork. They hadn't been there before, he was sure of it. He stuck his head through the window and studied the misty yard outside. It seemed to be deserted. He frowned. They were somewhere in the grounds then. All he had to do was find them. And once again he ran his fingers over the loop of the garrotte in his pocket.

Kate grabbed Lessing none too gently by the arm and pushed him up against the wall of the building. As far as she could tell, the thug in the archway hadn't seen them yet and she breathed a sigh of relief for the increasing gloom of the winter's afternoon, which might now be their ally.

'Keep quiet and stick close to me,' she whispered into Lessing's ear, conscious of his trembles and the little whimpers he kept making, which could easily be picked up on the still air.

Almost dragging him, she edged her way along the wall to the basement laboratory and pulled him down the steps with her, pressing him against the wall at the bottom, with one hand cupped around his mouth as footsteps rang on the stone slabs above, then stopped at the top of the steps. She visualized sharp eyes peering down at the lighted laboratory windows and held her breath, watching white-coated figures moving about within the lab and praying that one of them wouldn't approach the window and peer out. Lessing quivered against her and emitted a soft terrified moan. She gripped his throat with her other hand and squeezed tightly, cutting off his air supply. Silence as he tried to claw the hand away.

She tightened her grip and felt his body sag against her.

There was a scraping sound from above and then the footsteps moved on. She released her grip on Lessing's throat, then slowly removed her hand cupped over his mouth. He exhaled in a long trembling gasp and sank down on to his knees, making rasping choking noises.

'Shut it!' she whispered in a hoarse voice. 'He'll hear you.'

In the laboratory one of the white coats crossed the room to the window and she ducked down beside the agency man, squeezing his shoulder tightly in warning as a shadow was projected on the wall beside them. She heard the faint clink of bottles and water spurted out of a pipe by her feet and into a small grating. The shadow vanished.

'Come on – quickly!' she breathed into Lessing's ear, then hauled him roughly to his feet and dragged him back up the steps.

'You nearly suffocated me,' he wheezed.

'That's nothing to what they'll do to you if they catch us,' she retorted. 'Now come on!'

The yard seemed deserted, but in the thickening mist it was difficult to be sure. Kate peered into the shadows. Where had the hulk gone? Back into the house via another door into an outbuilding or over to the parked horse boxes? She took a chance. 'Come on!' she said again and, grabbing Lessing by his shirt collar, all but jerked him off his feet.

They made the archway without mishap – there was no sign of anyone – and they had a clear run to the shrubbery at the front of the house. Concealed among the dripping bushes, however, Kate studied the firmly closed electronic front gate with a mounting sense of frustration. As she'd noted earlier, there didn't appear to be any surveillance cameras in the grounds and she hadn't heard the sound of any dogs, but getting clear of the house without detection seemed to be impossible.

The only way they would get through the gate was if

someone decided to go out, or the house received another visitor, which might give them a slim opportunity to slip away before the gate closed again. But in her heart of hearts she knew that the odds on that happening were about a hundred to one against. So what did they do? They couldn't hide in the shrubbery for ever and once daylight dawned, it wouldn't be long before they were found. No, they had to get out while it was dark – scale the wall if necessary – and she made a rueful grimace at the thought.

'What are we going to do?' Lessing suddenly whimpered beside her. 'How can we get out?'

'Good point!' she said sarcastically. 'I'm glad you raised it.'

'But – but we can't stay here all night. I'm cold and wet and I need my inhaler.'

As if to reinforce the fact, he went into a fit of raucous coughing.

She grabbed his arm tightly. 'Stop that!' she grated. 'They'll hear you.'

Now he was crying again, sobbing like a small child between rending coughs. 'I can't help it, I'm ill.'

Spinning him round on his haunches, she grabbed his face with both hands. 'If you don't shut up, I'll leave you to them. Then you won't need a bloody inhaler because you won't be breathing anymore.'

He was shaking violently now and for a moment she thought she might have gone too far. He was obviously terrified and maybe shock tactics only made things worse.

'Look,' she said with forced patience. 'You stay here and keep very quiet. I'm going to take a look around to see if I can find another way out—'

'You can't!' His hands were clutching at her coat in a panic. 'What if you don't come back?'

Gently, but firmly, she pulled his hands away. 'I won't leave you, I promise, but one of us has to do a recce. Do you want to do it?'

He shook his head quickly and she stood up. 'Just stay right here so I know where to find you – and for heaven's sake keep quiet.'

Before he could protest further she was gone, pushing her way through the shrubbery in the other direction, away from the gate.

The rain had stopped completely now, but the mist swirled around her like a live thing, cold, dank and smelling of stagnant water and decay.

Within a few yards, the shrubbery gave way to more lawn, stretching away between the front of the house, with its gravel forecourt, and the huge sheer wall encircling the property. Striking off to her left through the bushes, she kept her back to the house, skirting the lawn until the shrubbery ended and she found herself on the edge of a gravel path, which seemed to follow the line of the wall as it curved away from her towards the far side of the building. Darting across the path, she pressed herself against the wall and followed it along, all the time casting anxious glances across the lawn towards the fuzzy outline of the house. But nothing stirred and shortly afterwards the lawn gave way to more shrubbery effectively masking her from view.

She made faster progress after that, but she didn't get far. Within twenty or thirty yards the path ended again in a small paved area, with a small stone outhouse – a gardener's hut perhaps – backing on to the wall to her left and half-a-dozen refuse bins lined up against what was obviously the end wall of the house on her right. In front of her was an open archway and, checking it out, she found herself staring into the same paved yard she and Lessing had only just left. Her spirits sank. She had completed almost a full circuit of the house and all that she had managed to establish was that there seemed to be no way out of the grounds except via the main gate – or was there?

Spinning round, she focused on the stone outhouse. It had

actually been constructed against the perimeter wall and she could just see that the top of the wall was only about three feet above the outhouse roof. If she could get up on to that roof – maybe using the sill of the single window for the purpose – she could reach the top of the wall and lay her anorak over the barbed wire before climbing over. She had no idea what was on the other side, but it was worth the gamble – after all, what other option was there? First, though, she had to get back to Lessing and persuade him to follow her.

But she never got the chance. She didn't hear the soft footfalls behind her until the last minute and when she whirled round, the tall dark figure was just feet away, standing close to the wall of the house, staring at her.

For a moment she found herself incapable of movement, every muscle and sinew locking in a form of temporary paralysis and an icy worm burrowing deep into her gut. But then the figure stepped directly in front of her and she released a loud gasp in which both surprise and relief were equally mixed.

'Horse?' she exclaimed. 'Thank God! How the hell did you get here?'

The NCA man gave a hard laugh. 'Well, if it isn't the meddling plod,' he said. 'You never give up, do you?'

She shook her head quickly. 'We have to get out of here,' she said. 'They were holding a newsman, Gabriel Lessing, in the house. I managed to get him out and have him hidden near here.'

'Very resourceful of you.'

'Yes, well I need to go back for him. Then we can get over the wall from the roof of this outhouse.'

He nodded. 'Ellie Landy came to the same conclusion,' he replied.

Kate frowned. 'Ellie Landy? But how—'

'Did I know?' he finished for her. 'But I know everything.'

And he produced a small automatic pistol from somewhere,

which he levelled at her stomach. 'You should have listened to me at the start,' he said. 'Now it's all too late!'

CHAPTER 16

THE ASHTRAY ON DI Roscoe's desk was full and he had already started on another filter-tip. He had heard nothing from Hayden and it was now over four hours since Kate Lewis had last been seen. His duodenal ulcer was playing up, he had run out of chewing gum and, to make a bad situation even worse, the DCI was still refusing to allow a full-blown search because of the resource implications and the risk of being accused by the headquarters hierarchy of crying wolf.

Roscoe could have tried to go over his head, but he doubted whether that would have received a sympathetic response in the relevant quarters or achieved anything in the long run – especially if Kate Lewis had then turned up safe and well. The trouble was, whichever way he chose to jump – to await the result of Hayden's house to house inquiries a while longer, or to try and send the balloon up now and initiate a full-blown search – he was likely to be criticized by the top level brass and dumped on by his career-obsessed boss, whose chameleon-like qualities had become almost legendary.

He didn't hear the knock on his office door at first, but when the wizened detective constable knocked again, he jerked out of his reverie with a grunt. 'What?'

'There's a DCI from the NCA on his way to see you, sir,' the DC announced cheerfully. 'Sounded a bit pissed off on his mobile.'

'Thanks,' Roscoe responded gloomily. 'Any more good news for me?'

The DC was right about the visitor's mood – Detective Chief Inspector Justin Hart was certainly not very happy.

'My department has a problem,' he said, after introducing himself, and he flashed a gold Rolex watch on his wrist as he shook hands with the DI before dropping into a chair in front of his desk.

Roscoe studied Hart's tanned complexion and the sleek, styled black hair that just covered his ears and scowled, reading high-flying golden boy in every crease of the expensive-looking designer suit and black Italian shoes. 'You have a problem?' he echoed drily. 'Try mine for size.'

Hart grimaced, unimpressed by the DI's cynical witticism. 'I gather you have been in touch with one of my DIs about an operation we're running on your manor?' he queried.

Roscoe nodded, elbows on the table and eyes narrowed over steepled fingertips. 'The drugs thing?' he said.

Hart gave him an old-fashioned look. 'The drugs thing,' he agreed. 'But it's a bit more than just a "drugs thing".' We are dealing with a powerful international syndicate run by—'

'The so-called Sandman,' Roscoe finished for him.

'The Sandman, yes. You're obviously well-briefed.'

Roscoe grunted. 'Yeah, but not well enough.'

Hart picked up the hostile vibes immediately and treated him to a brief rueful smile. 'I realize you should have been told about the op at the start, and I apologize for that, but unfortunately secrecy was vital, because we had an undercover officer on the ground and we couldn't afford to jeopardize his safety.'

'Larry Gittings,' Roscoe responded. 'Otherwise known as Horse.'

'Exactly, Larry Gittings – whom I believe you have already met?'

'In a manner of speaking, yes – not that he told us a lot,

apart from insulting one of my detective sergeants, that is.'

Hart winced. 'Sorry about that and I'm afraid it is him that I am here about.'

'Go on.'

The DCI squirmed a little in his chair. 'Our operation started in the Met – Pimlico to be precise – about four months ago when info came to our notice through a reliable snout that a powerful new criminal syndicate had moved into the area and was taking over the manufacture and supply of a whole variety of Class A and B narcotics from other key players. A number of drug-related murders took place and several known premises were fire-bombed during the turf war that followed. Accordingly, we set up a specialist crime unit to deal with the threat posed by the syndicate – adopting zero tolerance tactics to lean on suspected gang members, raiding clubs and known haunts and also employing sophisticated information gathering and surveillance techniques—'

Roscoe waved a hand irritably. 'OK, OK, spare me the crap. You don't need to teach Grandma to suck eggs – I've been in the job long enough to know the process – and I guess you made the Smoke too hot for the new boys, so the Sandman moved everyone out to the sticks, where it was quieter.'

'Er – yes, precisely, and he set up the Sapphire Club as the street contact point for the buyers representing the country's big dealers, arranging for the order and supply of bulk supplies of narcotics through their representatives, paid for by way of sophisticated money-laundering transfers.'

'Why not just use the Dark Web? It's all the rage now, according to the news.'

'Not enough potential as yet, we suspect. He's a major player and prefers the traditional methods of trafficking.' He sighed. 'Anyway, the fact is our operation finally got a breakthrough. One of our highly experienced undercover officers—'

'Larry Gittings?'

'Larry Gittings – reported to us that he was on the verge

of infiltrating the organization through his association with one of their front men—'

'Leroy Joseph?'

Hart was clearly caught on the back foot. 'You *are* well briefed, Mr Roscoe. But yes, you are exactly right. Joseph had no idea who Gittings was, of course, but he came to trust him as another dealer who wanted an "in" with the syndicate and he made quite a bit of money on the side by supplying Gittings with whatever he claimed to need—'

'Which, hopefully, Gittings then passed to a secure police depository.'

Hart was squirming again. 'That's what happened initially, yes, and Gittings sent regular reports on his progress to a handler we had installed in a house in Glastonbury.'

'And?'

'Well, the reports he submitted gradually started to become vaguer and the deposits of illegal material which we expected him to obtain in order to maintain his cover then dried up. We got the impression he was stalling for some reason.'

'But your DI said nothing about this when we made contact with your unit to verify his bona fides?'

Hart made a face and examined a crease in his trousers with two manicured fingers. 'Er – no, but we couldn't. At that stage, we assumed Gittings had encountered a problem, which, for professional reasons, he didn't want to admit to, and would ultimately find a solution and deliver the goods.'

'So you said nothing?'

'We – er – decided on a policy of wait and see.'

'You could have pulled him out?'

'Yes, but that would have compromised the whole operation and wasted months of effort – not to mention the loss of a key target villain.'

'So why are you here now?'

Hart seemed unwilling to meet Roscoe's belligerent stare.

'It – it was felt that the local force should be made aware of our concerns.'

But Roscoe was well ahead of him and he leaned forward in his chair, his big hairy hands clenched on the desk top and his eyes practically lazering his perspiring colleague. 'He's gone AWOL, hasn't he?' he accused. 'You think he's been turned and you've lost him?'

Hart swallowed hard again. 'We think it is possible, yes.'

Roscoe swore savagely. 'Shit sticks! And that bastard had the audacity to come in here and carry on with the con, while your lot effectively aided him by keeping shtum! Well, for your information, I've now got a missing DS who may have blundered into the whole filthy mess. What do you suggest I do about that, you pathetic arsehole?'

But Detective Chief Inspector Justin Hart had no answer to that!

'Why?' Kate demanded, staring at the pistol in Horse's hand. 'You are a copper, like me.'

Her mind was once more in overdrive, trying to think her way out of her current predicament, but finding herself focusing instead on the pistol levelled at her chest. She had no idea whether they had found Gabriel Lessing yet but she knew that, even if they hadn't, he would have about as much chance of getting out of this place on his own as she had of overpowering the NCA man.

Gittings gave a hollow laugh. 'No, love,' he replied, 'I'm not like you. I'm a realist. The authorities will never be able to stop illegal drugs trafficking, I realized that a long time ago. There will always be a market for the stuff and where there's a market, there are people who will always be prepared to produce and sell whatever is in demand. It's called the market economy.'

'So, in your book, it's a case of, if you can't beat them, join them?'

'Something like that, yes, and it is way better than waiting another fourteen years for a measly police pension.'

'Even if it involves murdering innocent people on the way – like Ellie Landy and the girl, Polly, for instance?'

He snorted. 'I had nothing to do with Ellie Landy's murder and I don't know anything about the death of this Polly girl either. My role has always been simply to frustrate the police operation – keep the NCA off the Sandman's back – nothing more than that. I've stiffed no one.'

'But you're still part of the same filthy business, so you're just as much to blame for their deaths as your scumbag friends are, even if you didn't actually do the business.'

He released his breath in a loud hiss. 'Ellie Landy asked for all she got. She wouldn't leave things alone – kept poking her nose into matters that didn't concern her – became a real pain, just like you.'

'I'm glad I proved to be a pain.'

'Oh you've been a pain all right and I've done everything I could think of to stop you becoming so much of a pain that it was decided to take you out altogether.'

'How very noble of you. So what happens now – if I didn't but know?'

He shrugged. 'That's up to the Man—'

'What, the nice Mr Pavlović?'

He stiffened. 'How do you know his name?'

'I know a lot of things – like Pavlović's thug, Tommy, stiffing Leroy a short time ago, for example. Did you help Tommy get rid of the body, I wonder?'

'Leroy?' He was plainly shaken by the news. 'You've got it wrong. Leroy is Mr Pavlović's right-hand man.'

'Not anymore he isn't. He was apparently doing some dealing on his own account and Tommy made sure he didn't do it again.'

Gittings digested the information for a moment, before shaking his head quickly and apparently dismissing it. 'Then he was a fool and got what he deserved.'

'You really believe that?'

'A hundred percent,' he replied, though his tone lacked conviction.

'Good for you,' she sneered, "cause you're probably the next one on Pavlović's hit list.'

He sighed a little too casually and she sensed a new tightness in his manner. 'Nice try, Kate, but it won't work. Now let's go. Mr Pavlović is very keen to meet you.'

He stepped away from her and indicated with a flick of his pistol that she should proceed ahead of him through the archway. 'After you, and remember, I'll be right behind you.'

Kate stayed put. 'And if I refuse? Are you going to pull the trigger yourself? You know, dirty your own lily-white hands for a change and waste one of your colleagues?'

He nodded. 'I'm in this thing too deep to get out now, Kate, and you stopped being one of my colleagues when I made the decision to change sides. So, have no illusions – I will pull the trigger, if that's what it takes – put a round in your thigh maybe. It won't kill you but it'll hurt like hell! It's your choice.'

For a moment Kate continued to stand her ground but then he lowered his pistol a fraction and she sensed the cold deliberation in his posture, which told her he was not bluffing.

'So, what's it to be?' he said softly. 'Common sense or a hole in the leg?'

It was her turn to shrug as she stepped past him through the archway. 'I hope your boss has put the kettle on,' she threw back over her shoulder. But her outward bravado belied her true feelings and, even as she marched ahead of him across the paved yard, a cold solid lump had already formed in the pit of her stomach.

Hayden was almost beside himself. He had tried several

of the cottages previously visited but no one had admitted to owning a boat. He had also called up control to seek support from the force helicopter, only to be advised that this required authority from the very top and, in any event, the resource – shared as it was between the Gloucestershire force and that of Avon and Somerset – was already attending a serious pile-up on the M5. As for the police support group's diving team, with its specialist marine craft, this had evidently been called to a missing child, believed drowned, in a lake near Churchill, so was completely tied up.

Tight-lipped and close to panic now, he rang control and finally got things moving with a call to the fire service, who offered to attend the scene and carry out a floodlight search of the fields. It took them nearly an hour to get to the rendezvous point that had been established however, and before they could launch their inflatable, the mist that had been developing for some time now came down with a vengeance, blotting out everything and rendering a search operation out of the question.

'Can you at least run me across to Lowmoor?' Hayden queried.

The senior fire officer shook his head. 'Sorry, mate,' he said, 'but that's a couple of miles and, in this mist, crossing those flooded fields with all the fences, hedgerows and other obstructions lurking beneath the surface would be much too dangerous for my crews.' He clapped Hayden on the shoulder. 'Best to wait until daylight,' he advised and ordered the inflatable back on to its trailer.

Refusing to give up, Hayden drove to the next village, looking for another resident with a boat – any sort of boat. He did find one almost immediately but only to face further disappointment when he asked to borrow it. 'In this mist?' the middle-aged man exclaimed. 'Not with my inflatable; it's far too dangerous and anyway, what do you expect to see when it's like this?'

Almost at his wits' end, the detective returned to his car. He had to admit it, unless someone could come up with some clever master plan, he was stuffed!

CHAPTER 17

THE ROOM WAS heavily curtained, lit only by a solitary stand-ard lamp and the dancing flames of a roaring log fire. Kate realized where she was when Horse prodded her through the doorway into the stiflingly hot interior after a peremptory knock. She had sheltered in the bathroom next door less than an hour before.

Unable to stop herself, she dropped her gaze to the carpet, looking for any sign of the stains Tommy had referred to after the brutal murder of Leroy, but saw nothing in the poor light save a deep dark pile.

The only occupant of the room seemed to be a man dressed in what looked like a dark suit. He was crouched over the fire, stirring the logs with a poker when they entered and the firelight gleamed on a thatch of thick silvery hair, swept back over his ears.

'Check her for a wire,' the man said without turning round, his voice soft, but heavily accented.

Horse nodded and, easing off her anorak, rummaged through the pockets, throwing her a critical glance when, in addition to the pocket torch she was carrying and her warrant card, he produced the tablets and powder she had taken from the laboratory, placing them carefully on a nearby coffee table. Next, dropping the coat on the floor, he ran his hands hesitantly, almost apologetically over the top half of her body, wincing as he undid the front of her blouse and examined the cups of her bra. Then, apparently satisfied, he stepped back. 'She's clean,' he said, but nodded towards the items on the coffee table. 'Except for those.'

The man by the fire straightened up and, turning, raised an eyebrow when his gaze fell on the powder and tablets. 'Tut-tut, Sergeant!' he said, his English perfect in spite of his accent. 'That was very naughty of you. You should be ashamed of yourself. What would that constitute on one of your police charge sheets – theft or maybe burglary?'

Kate didn't answer, but studied him intently. He had to be in his sixties, with a pencil-thin, slightly stooped frame and long thin arms. The incredibly pale aquiline features might have been carved from ivory and the cruel beak-like nose and thin lips were characteristics reminiscent of a predatory bird. But it was his eyes that held Kate's gaze. Whether it was a trick of the firelight or not, she couldn't be sure, but they appeared red, as if reflecting the flames themselves.

The man seemed to read her mind. 'Achromatosis, my dear,' he said. 'It is a congenital disorder, due to an absence of an enzyme called tyrosinase, which produces melanin in the body. You would no doubt crudely refer to me as an albino.'

'Or the Sandman,' Kate said in reply, showing no sense of embarrassment or self-consciousness in the knowledge that the man she was confronting was nothing more than a cold-blooded killer and a pedlar of misery.

He gave a soft musical laugh. 'And you, of course, are Kate Lewis,' he said, holding out one hand. 'Zoran Pavlović at your service.'

Kate made no effort to take it and he manufactured a sigh. 'There's no chance of our being friends, then? Even if I forgive you for stealing my stuff?'

She didn't answer and he shrugged. 'Never mind. We've got a little while to get to know each other anyway.'

'Why on earth do you think I would want to get to know you?'

He laughed again. 'Well, we might have something in common – you never know. I spent many years living in this country, perfecting my English, after my late parents fled here as refugees. Maybe we went to the same school or university or lived in the same neighbourhood at some time? We could even have rubbed shoulders on the odd occasion.'

'I doubt it. I am very careful who I mix with.'

He blew a silent whistle. 'Oh, you do have sharp teeth, don't you, Sergeant?'

He crossed the room and opened the door of a small cabinet, withdrawing two tumblers. 'Glass of whisky perhaps?' he said, placing the glasses on top of the cabinet and removing the glass stopper from a decanter already standing there.

'No thanks,' Kate said coldly. 'I don't drink with murderers.'

He half-turned, then poured two measures and handed one across to Gittings. 'You know, I do hate impoliteness, Horse,' he said. 'That's what's wrong with the young people in this country – no manners. In Serbia we treat people with respect.'

Kate snorted. 'Is that before or after you kill them?' she retorted, remembering the massacre at Srebrenica in the Bosnian war.

He ignored her response and, returning to his fireside, he dropped into an armchair, crossed his legs and studied her for a moment over the top of his glass.

'You have been quite a nuisance to me,' he said finally, 'just like that silly woman, Ellie Landy. It's because of her that I am soon going to have to pack up and leave this charming spot – and if it hadn't been for the damned floods, I'd have been long gone by now—'

'Ah, the horseboxes!' Kate cut in, suddenly cottoning on to the relevance of the two large lorries parked in the yard.

He nodded. 'Well spotted, Sergeant. Good cover, horseboxes. Police never check them and they are capable of holding not only my personal stuff, but all my lab kit, finished products and raw materials with ease. Brought everything here in them months ago when I quit London to set up my operation in Lowmoor. Trouble is, they're not exactly amphibious and there's too much stuff to risk moving it by boat, even though we have a nice inflatable in one of our barns for use in emergencies. So, unless I'm rumbled and have to use the inflatable, I am stuck here until the rain decides to stop and the Environment Agency start pumping everywhere out—'

'Surprised you chose to continue with an outdated street operation like this when you could have used the Dark Web instead,' Kate cut in. 'You wouldn't have needed a risky contact point, like the Sapphire Club, for your customers, simply a computer and a list of major dealers.'

He raised his eyebrows in admiration. 'You *are* well informed, my dear,' he acknowledged. 'Maybe I should be thinking of recruiting you to work for me, like Horse here. But you're right, the Dark Web is a lucrative market, and it may interest you to know that I *am* currently investigating its potential. But there is a lot to be said for the traditional old-fashioned street sales, particularly with the quantity of product that I am able to supply. I am not in the game of selling a few grams of cocaine or cannabis to some dissolute kids in Brixton or Moss Side. I run a multi-million pound business, funded by a syndicate of international backers, and supplying a wide variety of narcotic products to major dealers, and I have also set up a sophisticated channel for the regular provision of the raw materials I need, though unfortunately, because of the floods, I will be getting rather low on some things soon.'

'And meanwhile, there's every chance that your nasty little business will attract more unwelcome attention?' Kate said.

He raised one hand in a gesture of frustration. 'Exactly, my dear. You are so perceptive. And it has already happened. After Ellie Landy came, her fat boss turned up, then you

– who else might have suspicions and decide to drop in on me? After all, my good friend, Horse, here can only keep the NCA off my back for so long before they start getting restless and he has no influence at all with the press.'

He drained his glass and bent over the fire to pack on more logs from a basket beside the hearth. Then he turned to face Kate again and she saw him smile.

'Mind you,' he added, 'a bent copper is worth his weight in gold, because he knows all the angles. Horse's bosses still think he has infiltrated my organization by purporting to be a dealer, but in fact, he and I go back a long way, don't we, Larry? He was doing the business for me well before I moved in on the Met to set up my operation there. It's a very success-ful partnership.'

Kate snorted again. 'Yeah, until the NCA twig what's going on or another journalist gets a whisper about you from somewhere and decides to follow it up.'

'Unfortunately, that *is* a possibility,' he said. 'But at least I have you here now and the fat little journalist you released is trapped somewhere in the grounds of this house. My men will find him before long,' and he laughed, 'unless he can get over a nine foot high wall, like Ellie Landy, which I doubt in his poor physical condition.'

'He may surprise you,' she bluffed.

He shook his head. 'Oh, I doubt that, Sergeant. I have every confidence in him being found soon and I am looking forward to us resuming the little chat with him that you so rudely interrupted.'

'Like the chat you had with Ellie Landy before you killed her?'

He frowned. 'Actually, no, I never got to chat to poor Ellie, which was unfortunate. She broke in here, you see, much like you and Gabriel Lessing did, and discovered our state-of-the-art lab. When she was spotted, she took off in such a rush that she even left her mobile behind. She managed to scale the perimeter wall and took refuge in – of all places – the flooded crypt of our local church—'

'Where you deliberately drowned her.'

He tutted. 'What a terrible thing to say,' he exclaimed. 'What must you think of me?' He sighed. 'The truth is, she quite ferociously attacked Tommy when he found her down there, forcing him to defend himself. I gather that in the struggle she fell over on the steps and in trying to pacify her, Tommy didn't realize her head was under the water.' He shrugged. 'Very tragic.'

He was playing with her, that was obvious, and savouring every word of his farcical explanation. Kate shuddered, remembering what the pathologist had deduced from Ellie Landy's injuries, and picturing in her mind's eye the young woman lying on her back on those cold stone stairs, with the thug probably sitting astride her, holding her head under the water as she gasped for air and desperately clawed at the wall with her fingernails.

'You sound totally devastated,' she said with bitter sarcasm, adding, 'but at least you got to chat to Leroy before Tommy murdered him too – even if it was a bit of a one-sided conversation.'

Pavlović paused in the act of taking another sip from his glass. 'Leroy? Now how on earth could you know about that?'

He threw Gittings a searching glance, the insinuation in the glance unmistakable, but the detective had seen it coming. 'She told me about that,' he blurted, shaking his head quickly in panicky denial. 'I didn't know anything about it until then.'

Pavlović climbed slowly to his feet and ambled across the room to where she was still standing. 'Bit of a mystery girl, aren't you?' he said sibilantly. 'And we don't like mysteries, do we, Tommy?'

Kate hadn't heard the door open, but out of the corner of her eye she saw that a huge figure was standing just behind her.

'Now,' Pavlović said, 'we're going to play a little game, Sergeant. I'm going to ask you some questions about what you know and who you have told, and you're going to give me some straight answers. But there are quite unpleasant forfeits for you if I suspect you are feeding me a line – forfeits that Tommy here will impose with enthusiasm. OK?'

Kate didn't answer, but she was very aware of her legs shaking.

Pavlović peered into her face and she smelled the whisky on his breath. 'First question coming up then, my dear,' he said, treating her to another smile and glancing at his watch, 'and your starter for ten.'

Hayden was clearly shocked when he telephoned Roscoe and was told about Larry Gittings but he had more on his mind than a crooked policeman, and he came out with it almost immediately. 'I need a boat,' he exclaimed, 'to get to Lowmoor.'

Roscoe threw a quick glance at DCI Justin Hart before turning back to the phone. 'I realize that,' he said, 'but there's no way we can risk trying to cross flooded fields in this mist.' He peered out through the office window as he spoke, frowning at the white clouds of vapour swirling past the glass. 'It's pretty bad here too. The fire service were right. It would be much too dangerous because of possible submerged hazards.'

The DI heard Hayden's sharp hiss of frustration down the phone. 'So pull the chopper off its present commitment,' the DC continued. 'We can have an armed team in the village within half an hour.'

Roscoe snorted. 'An armed team? Grow up, Lewis. We have no grounds for that. Lowmoor is a rural village, not Dodge City!' He took a deep breath, thinking of his DCI's intransigence. 'Listen, I sympathize with your worries – I'm bloody worried too – but we have no real idea where Kate is or if in fact she is actually at risk from anyone—'

'So what about that bent copper, Gittings? What if she's fallen foul of him?'

'And what if she's just been delayed or held up by the mist? Her mobile could have died on her and we know the phone lines are down in that part of the country. We'd look bloody stupid if she turned up at the nick after we'd sent half the force down there to carry out a search.'

'OK, so have me dropped off there in the chopper with a couple of plods. We can at least start some inquiries.'

'No chance. The chopper was grounded when it returned from the M5 incident. The bad weather is pretty widespread apparently, with almost zero visibility because of the conditions. They won't be authorized to take off again until the morning and I've already spoken to the DCI and he reckons it's too early to hit the panic button, especially as your missus has done this sort of maverick "vanishing trick" thing before.'

'So what do we do in the meantime? Play cards?' Hayden shouted. 'We have a missing police officer, just in case you needed reminding, sir – a police officer who has been out of contact for four hours at least and who happens to be my wife! She could be in real trouble.'

Roscoe's eyes bulged as his slab-like face set in a ferocious scowl. 'Don't you think I realize that, you cheeky bastard?' he snarled. 'But the decision is out of my hands. So get your fat arse back to this office pronto, do you hear me?'

And he slammed the phone down with such force that a sheaf of papers on the edge of his desk flew off on to the floor.

Hart was plainly taken aback, but he obviously subscribed to the view that discretion was a lot better than valour and he said nothing for a few moments, instead studying Roscoe's belligerent expression and waiting for the over-stressed DI to calm down. It was a good move, for within a couple of minutes Roscoe's ferocious scowl reduced to a grimace and, as if suddenly making up his mind about something, he snapped to his feet.

'The insolent prick had a point though,' he growled with just a trace of reluctance. 'I need to see the boss and finally get something moving on this job.' He scowled again. 'And this time Ricketts is *going* to listen!'

Hart coughed discreetly. 'Want me to come in on it?' he queried.

Roscoe studied him in the manner of someone about to dismember an insect. 'Your mess,' he snarled. 'That's about the least you could do!'

Gabriel Lessing was crying again and he was too terrified to be ashamed of himself. It had to be well over half an hour since the woman police sergeant had left him in the shrubbery and she still had not returned. What on earth had happened to her? Had she been caught by the men who were looking for them – or, more likely, found a way out of the grounds and made off on her own? That's what he would have done in the circumstances, so it seemed a logical possibility.

Yes, that had to be it. She had run away and left him to it. The bitch!

He wiped a sleeve across his tear-stained face. He was on his own and he had to get a grip on himself. Crying and hyperventilating was not the answer; he had to try and think straight.

Footsteps in the gravel close by and a torch probed the mist swirling among the bushes sheltering him. He froze, biting his fist to stop himself crying out. There was a pregnant pause before the beam of the torch swung away from the spot and was swallowed up in the mist again. The footsteps moved on.

Lessing forced himself to stay still for what he judged to be another twenty minutes, then slowly stood up, parting the leaves of one of the shrubs and peering into the white nothingness. His legs were shaking fitfully and he was having difficulty getting his breath. But common sense told him he had to move. If he stayed where he was, it would only be a question of time before he was discovered – especially if the mist dispersed and let in the all-revealing moonlight. Well, the logic was OK, but leaving his hiding place was equally risky and he wasn't particularly keen on that idea either. In fact, it was at least another fifteen to twenty minutes before he finally plucked up the courage to make the move he knew he had to make.

Even then he wasn't a hundred percent convinced he was doing the most sensible thing and, feeling the solid surface of the driveway beneath his feet, he stopped short for a few moments, swallowing hard and peering fearfully to his left and then to his right. Nothing but clouds of mist – cold, damp and virtually impenetrable. He took a chance and turned right in the direction of the main gate, well aware from his first disastrous acquaintance with the house, where it was located.

As he crept through the mist, he couldn't help thinking about how badly he had managed things and how stupid he had been. He should have told the police everything instead of lying to them, but the prospect of securing a major scoop had been his all-consuming motivation and it had nearly cost him his life. Even now, he was not out of the woods. He still had to get through the main gate somehow – and then what? Like Ellie must have been before, he was trapped on an island with a gang of ruthless thugs looking for him. He should have thought about Kate Lewis then and what might have happened to her – after all, but for her, he would still have been roped to the wooden crate in the tower – but Gabriel Lessing was not a man to worry too much about other people; his concern had always been for himself and he wasn't about to change.

That concern made him especially careful now as the gate loomed up directly ahead – a fuzzy black slash seemingly floating towards him on a shifting swirling white sea. He had to be only a matter of feet away from it but he held himself in check. Maybe one of the thugs was already in position there, waiting for him to turn up? Slipping back into the shrubbery, he forced himself to remain there long enough to satisfy himself as much as he could that the mist was not concealing some shadowy figure. He saw nothing and finally stepped out of hiding and hurried quickly towards the gate.

As he'd expected, it was tightly secured and it was apparent that there was no way of opening the thing manually. Feeling his spirits sink as his panic started rising, he clenched his fists tightly in an effort to maintain control – and it was then that the badger materialized from the mist beside him and headed straight for the wall to one side of the gate!

Startled at first by the sudden appearance of the animal, he gaped at it in astonishment, but then he got an even bigger shock. The badger simply disappeared – not into the mist, but into the wall.

Gabriel Lessing may have been a coward, but there was nothing wrong with his brain and he cottoned on immediately.

A couple of strides brought him right up to the spot where the badger had disappeared and, dropping on to his hands and knees, he peered into the large hole which had been almost concealed behind a pile of rotting timber lying at the foot of the wall. It was close to one of the gate pillars where the stonework seemed to have collapsed in on itself at some time and the badger had no doubt widened it for his own personal use.

Wasting no time, Lessing clawed at the debris on either side of the hole, tearing his fingers on the broken blocks and rough pieces of cement until he had enlarged the hole sufficiently to thrust his head through. As if to provide some encouragement, the mist now cleared a little revealing the road beyond; he couldn't help moaning his excitement as he pulled more blocks out of the way.

The hole was then just big enough for his purposes and, heedless of the jagged edges tearing at him as he squeezed into it, he forced himself through on to the sodden grass verge that lay beyond. He was out. He could hardly believe it – he was *out*! Lessing had never believed in God – or any other deity for that matter – but he threw a muttered prayer at the heavens anyway, and, scrambling to his feet, took off at a shambling run in the direction of the village main street, a free man at last.

It was only when he had passed the closed and shuttered pub and found himself ankle deep in water that it dawned on him that, while he might have escaped from the house, he was still trapped in the village by the flooded fields. But then he saw the motorized rubber dinghy on the grass bank where Kate had left it and closer inspection revealed that it was not only equipped with an electric start but the all-important key had been carelessly left in the ignition. Straightaway, he knew fate had thrown him another lifeline. He had never operated an outboard motor before, but he reasoned that it was unlikely to be that difficult. The mist swirling just above the dark water which slopped around his feet couldn't have looked less inviting. A moment's reflection, however, convinced him he had no choice; falling into the floodwater would be unpleasant, but he could swim after a fashion and it was infinitely preferable to staying in Lowmoor.

Pulling the inflatable away from the bank into the water, he spent a few minutes trying to crank the engine as the dinghy drifted out from the shore. Then suddenly, with a throaty roar, it burst into life and he was in business.

CHAPTER 18

'QUESTION ONE,' PAVLOVIĆ said, studying Kate's face intently. 'How did you get here?'

Lying about the dinghy was pointless and simply risked giving Tommy standing behind her the excuse to inflict some pain, so Kate shrugged and answered truthfully. 'In a borrowed inflatable.'

'Where did you leave it?'

'On the grass, not far from the pub.'

'Excellent,' Pavlović acknowledged. 'We will check that out, of course.'

Kate met his gaze with a defiant stare, but said nothing. She guessed Tommy was pretty disappointed by her straight answer.

'Who lent you the dinghy?'

She tensed, knowing full well that if she revealed the name of the owner she would not only be signing the boy's death warrant, but that of his mother as well; Pavlović was about silencing all witnesses in the chain, not just herself.

'No one lent me it. I found it left on a verge and just took it.'

Pavlović sighed and shook his head. 'Sorry, but I don't believe you.'

She felt Tommy stir behind her and she blurted a desperate assurance.

'It's the truth. Why would I lie about something like that?'

'So how did you manage to start it without a key?'

She hesitated a second. 'The key had been left in it.'

Pavlović considered her reply for a moment, his strange eyes hooded and thoughtful. 'How convenient for you,' he commented, then added sibilantly, 'You have a pretty face and, I am sure, just as pretty a body. It would be a pity if Tommy had to spoil either.'

'I'm telling you the truth.'

He nodded slowly, then treated her to another smile. 'Question four,' he said. 'Who knows you are here?'

Her defiance re-surfaced in a desperate bluff, burying her fear. 'My boss and most of my team. They'll be on your back before you know it.'

His smile developed into a sneer. 'So, no one, eh? I guessed as much. You see, my dear, I know from what Horse here told me about you earlier that you are a bit of a lone wolf. You have a reputation for going it alone.' He shook his head and tutted several times. 'Very bad practice, that. Now, question five. Where is Gabriel Lessing? Where did you hide him?'

Kate thought quickly, then blurted, 'I got him out of the house, but we lost each other in the mist – I don't know where he is now.'

'Oh dear,' and Pavlović tutted again. 'I do believe we're getting into forfeits.'

There was a barely perceptible nod from him and Kate gasped as her blouse was suddenly ripped apart from behind, falling down to her waist. Then Tommy's meat-hooks closed over her arms in a vice-like grip, holding her rigidly in front of his huge body.

Returning to the fireplace almost nonchalantly, the albino bent down and withdrew the poker from among the blazing logs and blew on the smoking orange tip.

'Now,' he said, advancing towards her with the poker held out in front of him, 'let me ask you question five again.'

Gittings, silent up to this moment, took a pace forward, his eyes blazing. 'There's no need for this.'

Pavlović turned slowly to face him. 'What's up, Horse?' he asked with quiet menace. 'Getting squeamish in your old age?'

Gittings stopped short. 'No,' he muttered, once more cowed by the other's presence. 'It's just that—'

Pavlović's eyes seemed to burn into him. 'Tell you what,' he said. 'Why don't you do it, eh?'

Kate felt her legs start to buckle under her, as her eyes became riveted on the poker, which Pavlović carefully set down on a small coffee table, with the orange tip projecting over the edge and the handle turned towards Gittings.

'There you are, Horse,' Pavlović continued. 'It's all yours. Choose your spot but I would suggest that a touch just below the stud in her navel should do the trick.'

Whether or not Gittings would actually have picked up the poker and complied with his boss's instruction was never put to the test, for it was at this point that a series of loud knocks sent him striding to the door. There was a muffled excited conversation, then he swung back into the room. 'The boys have found a hole in the perimeter wall,' he said.

Pavlović glared at him. 'A hole?'

'Yeah, right beside the main gate, of all places, and they think Lessing has used it to escape.'

The albino's face contorted into an evil mask. 'Get after him!' he snarled. 'You too. He mustn't get off this island.'

As Gittings left the room at a run, Pavlović swung back to face Kate. 'You think you've won, don't you, Sergeant?' he rasped. 'Well, think again.' He stared over her shoulder. 'Put her upstairs in the tower room, Tommy,' he snapped. 'And stay with her until I decide how to dispose of her.' He thrust his face close to Kate's, the sour whisky smell enveloping her. 'And you can be sure, Sergeant,' he promised, 'that I will come up with something particularly imaginative.'

*

Gabriel Lessing was lost. He had got away from Lowmoor all right, but in the thick mist, he had no idea where he now was. Although he had started out on what should have been the main road, the hedgerows on either side of him had disappeared at one point and he had had to steer the dinghy in what he thought was the right direction. For all he knew, though, he could have drifted out into one of the adjoining fields and be heading entirely the wrong way. Twice he had scraped over something submerged just below the surface of the water and once he had cannoned into another line of half-buried hedgerow. Fortunately, however, the tough skin of the inflatable had remained intact – which was just as well, since, although he could swim after a fashion, he didn't fancy his chances in that cold grey water, marooned in the mist.

He had felt a brief spasm of guilt about leaving the police sergeant to her fate – especially as she had got him out of that awful house in the first place, but faced with the dangers posed by the submerged patchwork of fields he was forced to navigate he had soon put thoughts of Kate Lewis out of his mind. After all, she was a police officer and risk was what police officers were paid for, wasn't it? Maybe he would ring Highbridge police station about her once he got back to where he had left his Volvo, using the spare mobile he kept in the glove-box. That would enable him to discharge his responsibilities as a public-spirited citizen without having to subject himself to the long drawn-out process of interview, which a personal visit to the police station would entail. He'd then be free to return to his lodgings to pack, before heading hot-foot back to his office in the Smoke. Perfect!

With Kate Lewis consigned to his subconscious, he started thinking about the sensational piece he was going to write as soon as he was back in London – a story so hot that he felt sure he could virtually name his price for an exclusive with one of the big nationals. He would tart the whole thing up, of course – highlight his own heroic pursuit of the truth about 'poor' Ellie Landy's death and his daring escape from the clutches of a ruthless criminal gang – but the story had the potential to be a massive headliner in its own right and, despite his fears for his own safety in the choking mist, he could hardly control his excitement.

He was still thinking about what his scoop would mean to him and his tottering business when the hazy outline of the row of cottages materialized ahead of him and slightly to his right. Slowing the inflatable's growling outboard, he peered intently through the swirling white clouds to try and see if he was returning to the spot where he had boarded the supply boat earlier or whether the inflatable had taken him somewhere else. Either way, it didn't really matter. It was enough to get safely back to dry land, and if he happened to be in the wrong place, so what? He could always get someone to take him back to where he had left his car.

As it turned out, however, the fates were still with him. Seconds later, the dinghy grounded on something beside a familiar wooden fence bordering the main road where it disappeared into the floodwater. He had been delivered right back to his point of departure.

Killing the outboard engine, he scrambled out of the inflatable into calf-deep water and, without bothering to secure it, stumbled up a slight incline into the side road which cut off from the main drag along the edge of the flooded fields in front of a row of stone cottages.

He took no notice of the cottages or Hayden's plain CID car parked in a shallow layby just past the last in the row – he had more important things on his mind – and he was relieved to find his Volvo exactly where he had left it seemingly an eternity ago. The thugs who had incarcerated him had not bothered to take his car keys off him when they had seized his mobile and he produced the remote with the theatrical aplomb of a man whose worries were now all behind him. Gabriel Lessing was finally going to make his mark on society and earn the fame he had been denied for so long – at least, that is what he thought.

Kate was very frightened. Tommy had hardly taken his eyes off her since wheeling her up into the very tower room from which, ironically, she had earlier sprung Gabriel Lessing. It wasn't just a look either. It was the intense devouring stare of a ravenous animal, but an animal that was obsessed with something far removed from food. With her anorak back on and securely zipped up after her terrifying experience downstairs, she was nevertheless conscious of the fact that underneath it her blouse hung in tatters around her and although she was completely covered, under Tommy's penetrating stare she had the disturbing, unreal feeling that he could see right through the fabric.

She was relieved that Lessing seemed to have made good his escape, but was under no illusions as to what that would mean for her. The little wimp was too preoccupied with his own welfare to worry much about the lady cop who had risked her neck to effect his release. Though she prayed that if by some fluke he managed to get clear of Lowmoor and make it to the nearest village his natural cowardice would send him straight to the nearest police station, she realized there was also every chance that he would do nothing and just keep on going.

No, she had to face facts. Even if Lessing had managed to get away, she couldn't rely on him to send help; she was on her own and her time was almost up. She had to get out of this room before either Lessing was found or Pavlović finally gave up on him and was forced to cut his losses, for then her life would not be worth a dime.

That realization sent her brain into near panic-stricken overdrive as she desperately tried to think her way out of her dire situation. It was obvious that Tommy was not going to walk away and leave her locked up in the room. He had been told by Pavlović to stay with her and it was obvious that he was going to comply with those instructions to the letter. But so confident was he in his physical prowess that he hadn't even bothered to lock the door behind him and that did at least present her with a chance, albeit a slim one, if she could just manage to work out a way of distracting him.

Studying that hard brutish face, however, and reading the blatant message in the tiny blue eyes that covered her like twin pistol barrels she shuddered. The one option that had occurred to her couldn't have been more risky and the very thought of what she would have to do filled her with absolute revulsion. But desperate situations called for equally desperate measures and she wasn't blessed with the luxury of choice – coupled with which, something had presented itself to her to spur her on.

By chance her fingers had brushed against the cold steel of the pocket knife she had used to cut Lessing's bonds and which, amazingly, she had left behind in her panic to get him out of the tower room. The knife was now lodged between the slats of the box on which she sat and its blade was still in the open position. Only a couple of inches long, it nevertheless provided her with an opportunity she could not ignore.

Taking a deep breath, she slowly unzipped her anorak, allowing it to fall open and with it the remnants of her blouse. Tommy's eyes flickered slightly.

'I know what you want,' she said, trying to keep her voice steady.

Tommy grinned, exposing a row of broken teeth. 'Do you?' he said.

She nodded and stood up. 'You can have it if you agree to let me go,' she said, knowing full well that there was no chance of that and praying he would not see through her contrived naïvety and suspect a trick.

But he was too obsessed with his carnal desires to suspect anything and he ran his tongue across his lower lip in anticipation. 'Why don't I just take it anyway?' he sneered, moving a step closer.

She shook her head this time, feigning shock at what she had known all along would be his response and shrinking back against the crate. At the same time she fumbled behind her for the knife. 'No – no, not unless we have a deal.'

He snorted his derision. 'You're in no position to make deals, lady,' he pointed out, 'just in case you hadn't noticed.'

He took another couple of steps towards her – a giant of a man, well over six foot in height and built like a brick shed, a crescent-shaped scar down one side of his face and what looked like old stitch marks from a bottle injury across his bald scalp. She felt sick. What chance did she have against this huge powerful thug who had already killed at least two people?

But it was too late for second thoughts now, for he was towering over her, trapping her against the crate, his thick wet lips curled in a lecherous grin and a thin trail of saliva running from a corner of his mouth down his chin. As his left hand closed over her right breast and his right slid down inside the front of her trousers, she brought her knee up savagely between his legs. But it was apparent that he had been expecting this and deflected the blow with a twist of his knee, bursting into a roar of laughter at the futility of such an obvious response.

'You'll have to do a lot better than that, lady,' he taunted – which is exactly what she did. What he had not suspected was that the move had actually been a diversionary tactic and he was totally unprepared for the follow-up. The pocket knife clasped tightly in Kate's hand swung in a deadly arc towards him, slashing through his right cheek and opening it up to the bone.

The effect on Tommy was predictable. With a wild almost feminine scream, he stumbled backwards, both hands flying to his face in a futile defensive gesture as he cannoned into the wall, fountains of blood spurting everywhere, like the discharge from a fractured water pipe. Kate made the most of the situation, ducking under his arms and racing for the door. She heard him wheeling round behind her, lumbering in pursuit despite his injuries and hurling threats and foul abuse after her as she wrenched the door open.

She took the narrow staircase two at a time, almost losing her balance twice on the uneven steps before she gained the corridor below – at which point she stopped short, staring wildly about her. Where to now?

Heavy footsteps on the stairs behind her. 'Bitch,' Tommy yelled. 'I'll rip your guts out!'

It had to be the ground floor and the toilet window she had used before; it was the only way she knew.

She turned left towards the main staircase, fearing that at any moment Tommy might produce a pistol and put a bullet in her back. But he didn't and within a few yards she was out of his line of sight as she threw herself down the stairs, blind panic pushing her on at a reckless breakneck speed – the thought of the thug racing after her enough of an incentive to keep going.

She reached the floor below well ahead of him – a quick glance over her shoulder satisfying herself that he was not in sight. Maybe she had lost him, maybe he had turned right in the corridor above and was even now checking the wrong floor and heading in entirely the wrong direction? After all, how could he know about the toilet and that all-important insecure window?

But then she heard a shout and the thud of feet on the stairs behind her once more. Somehow he had sensed where she had gone and, like a bloodhound, was sticking to the scent. She forced herself to run faster.

Her heart seemed to be leaping about inside her chest like a live thing, the perspiration pouring down her face and neck when she finally stumbled through the toilet door. The mist was clearing outside and moonlight now illuminated the room again, revealing that the window was closed. She clambered up on to the toilet seat and tugged on the cup-handle to pull it up. It stirred, but refused to open, apparently jammed. Hell's bells, there was no time!

Footsteps now in the corridor behind her. Tommy! She was trapped! She rushed back to the toilet door to shut it, feeling for a key in the metal lock as she did so. There wasn't one. Her mouth was dry, her head spinning.

'Got you!' a harsh voice snarled and she saw a shadow through the gap as she slammed the door in the thug's face and put her foot against the bottom of it. Then her questing fingers found the bolt. It seemed to be only a cheap antiquated thing, probably only held on by two or three screws, but it snapped home a fraction of a second before Tommy put his shoulder against the door.

Kate tried not to think about how long the bolt would hold, but sprang back across the room to the toilet seat, clambering up on it and using all her strength to haul on the window's cup-handle. The window rose an inch, then jammed again. Behind her, the toilet door was shaking under Tommy's maniacal assault and she heard a splintering sound as the bolt started to separate from the frame. She was shaking now, crying out in tearful frustration and hauling on the cup-handle with a kind of futile desperation. She was going to die, just like Ellie Landy, but worse. Tommy would rape her first and then take his time killing her, and there was nothing she could do to stop him.

As the bolt on the toilet door finally flew off and hit the floor with a metallic 'clink', she forced her fingers under the partially open window and hauled upwards in one last ditch effort – and it was then that the window suddenly shot up as if propelled by a spring, admitting the cold damp air of the marsh.

Tommy got to her as she scrambled through the gap,

grabbing the hem of her anorak. But in his weakened blood-ied state he was no match for her and when the heel of her left foot smashed into his badly injured face, he was forced to let go with an agonized cry, overbalancing and pitching back-wards on to the toilet floor, leaving Kate to stumble off into emerging strands of moonlight – free at last but for how long?

CHAPTER 19

HAYDEN WAS SITTING in the CID car, staring dismally at the clouds of white mist, feeling totally helpless and frustrated. He had no intention of returning to Highbridge nick as he had been instructed to do by Roscoe, but deep down he couldn't help asking himself what on earth he hoped to achieve just sitting there in the cold car, staring at nothing. True, the mist *had* thinned a little, but not enough to enable him to get things moving, so all he could do was to sit there, staring at it and desperately praying for it to disappear completely.

His prayers were not immediately answered, but as his spirits hit rock-bottom, he suddenly heard the growl of an engine. Frowning, he pressed closer to the windscreen, wiping a hand across the partially clouded glass and clearing a small space through which he was able to see a few feet of roadway in front of the car. He strained his eyes, looking for what sounded like an approaching motorcycle. But he saw nothing even though the engine seemed very close. Then it dawned on him that the sound was not coming from the roadway in front of him but from his left and the direction of the flooded fields. A boat – it had to be a boat and that distinctive growl was more than likely produced by an outboard motor. He felt a sudden surge of excitement. A boat – at last he was in with a chance.

Grabbing his torch and throwing open the door of the CID car, he hauled himself out on to the roadway and stumbled blindly in the direction of the approaching engine, just as it died in a choking gasp what had to be only a few feet away. Seconds later he caught a glimpse of a fuzzy shadow, cutting through the swirling vapour, directly across his path, before abruptly vanishing again.

For one glorious moment he thought it might be Kate, on her way to where she had left her car after bringing the borrowed dinghy back but then cruel common sense prevailed. He had only been afforded the briefest of glimpses of the figure in the murk and had not been able to tell whether it was that of a man or a woman, but he had seen enough to know that the build was all wrong – Kate was tall and slim, this character was short and dumpy. Nevertheless, he was determined to find out who it was and what they were doing in a boat on the flooded Levels and he broke into a run, plunging into the mist after them.

He heard the crack of remotely operated electronic door locks and saw the orange flash of a vehicle's front indicators just as he reached the big Volvo car and he managed to grab the driver's door to prevent it being closed behind the rotund little man who was climbing behind the wheel. Hayden recognized him immediately, despite the mist curling in round the interior light, and quickly reached inside the car to snatch the key from the ignition.

Gabriel Lessing cringed in his seat, releasing a series of sobs. 'Please,' he whimpered, 'don't hurt me. I won't say anything, really I won't.'

It was obvious that he didn't recognize Hayden from the interview at Highbridge police station, but his pathetic pleas sent a neon alert flashing in the CID man's brain.

'Won't say anything about what, Mr Lessing?' he queried with a heavy frown.

Lessing's jaw dropped as recognition suddenly dawned and with it an abrupt change in demeanour.

'Give me back my key,' the agency man snarled

straightening up. 'You have no right—'

Hayden leaned further into the car, his intimidating bulk crushing Lessing into the seat. 'I asked you a question,' he said softly. 'Won't say anything about what?'

Lessing flinched again, his new-found bravado abruptly evaporating. 'I don't want any trouble,' he blurted. 'I just want to go home.'

Hayden released his breath in an explosive hiss. 'I am not a violent man, Mr Lessing,' he said, 'but I am beginning to lose patience with you, so you had better come clean right now. Where have you just come from and what won't you say anything about?'

Lessing gulped. 'They – they locked me in a room,' he whined. 'They would have killed me but for that woman sergeant. I – I only just got out in time.'

Hayden stiffened and knelt on the edge of the seat. 'I think you'd better tell me everything,' he said harshly, 'especially what you know about my wife.'

Which the press man did immediately, his reluctance totally shot away now – the whole story spilling out of him in a garbled rush.

'And you left Kate there after she'd got you out?' Hayden choked when he'd finished. 'You ran out on her?'

'There was nothing I could do,' Lessing lied. 'I was going for help.'

Hayden glared at him, his face ashen. 'You despicable little worm,' he snarled, hauling himself back out of the car. 'If anything's happened to her, you'd better start looking for somewhere to hide your miserable carcass.' He held up the ignition key he had seized. 'Meanwhile you can start walking.' Raising his arm and pivoting round, he hurled the keys as hard as he could into the mist and was rewarded by a faint plop as they hit water.

Heedless of the bleating protests that chased after him, he headed back across the roadway at a run. Lessing had not bothered to pull the dinghy up on to the grass and, even as Hayden caught sight of the rubber prow, the thing had already begun to drift away from the bank. He lurched forward and grabbed the rope trailing over the grass, pulling the craft back in. Then, snaking the rope over a broken fence post projecting above the water close to where the main road disappeared, he secured it with a hitch and climbed aboard.

Fortunately Lessing had also left the key in the ignition and the engine was still hot. It started after a couple of coughs and, well familiar with sailing dinghies from his time at public school and after that as a member of a local club, he had no difficulty turning the boat in the right direction. Seconds later he was a grey phantom disappearing into the mist, steering one-handed while he gripped the torch tightly under his arm as he jabbed the keys of the pad on his mobile with the thumb of his other hand.

The meeting in DCI Ricketts' office was acrimonious, with both Ricketts and Roscoe on the defensive and continually sniping at each other over Kate Lewis's disappearance. Hart did his best to cool things down, but only succeeded in drawing the hostility back on himself and the NCA for keeping their suspicions about Larry Gittings quiet for so long. Only when the crackling mobile phone call came through did the atmosphere change and the two DCIs listened with rapt attention to what was for them a heated one-sided conversation between Roscoe and the mystery caller.

'Another problem?' Hart queried when the DI slammed the phone down again.

Roscoe eyed him grimly. 'You could say that,' he growled. 'That was Hayden Lewis. It seems he may have found where your so-called Sandman is holed up and also where Kate Lewis could have been heading when she disappeared.'

'Where is he now?'

Roscoe snorted. 'On his way to some manor house in

Lowmoor. Bloody fool thinks he's Superman and, if what he says is kosher, he'll need a damned-sight more than blue tights and the power of flight to get out in one piece.'

Ricketts gulped. 'This could provoke a major incident. The Chief Super will go spare.'

Roscoe's eyes glittered. 'Then maybe you should warn him what's going down before it happens, *sir*,' he said, 'and while you're about it, you might like to suggest he gets on to head-quarters PDQ to request specialist support and some armed backup.'

Grabbing his coat from the back of the chair and with Hart in tow, he stomped out of his office, snapping at the detective constable sitting at one of the desks in the general office to join him as he headed for the main doors. Out in the police station yard a few seconds later, he tossed the car keys to the DC. 'Let's go hunting,' he growled. 'We've got a DS to find.'

The DC glanced upwards. 'Looks like we'll have some help too, sir,' he said.

Following his gaze, the DI allowed himself a grim smile of satisfaction. He had already suspected that the mist was starting to thin and the confirmation was right there above his head in the form of the pale smoky face of a slowly emerging moon.

Hayden saw the face of the moon appear through a hole in the mist at about the same moment as Roscoe and minutes later glimpsed the dark hump of Lowmoor through the tattered white clouds dissolving in front of him. It was only then that the scale of the task he had set himself really dawned on him.

How on earth was he going to achieve it single-handed? OK, so from what Lessing had said, Kate had sprung him from a room in a big manor house at the far end of the village and there couldn't be many big manor houses in a place the size of Lowmoor. But locating the premises was the easy part. Getting inside promised to be a lot more difficult and, even if he managed it, he still had to find Kate and there was no way of knowing whether she was hiding somewhere in the grounds, had succeeded in getting out, like Lessing, or had, in fact, been taken by the Sandman's thugs.

Not for the first time in his life, he regretted his impetuosity. He should have waited for Roscoe and the troops to arrive before doing anything, but true to form where Kate was concerned, he had allowed his heart to rule his head, and it was too late for regrets now; he just had to get on with the job as best he could and hope for the best. As if to reinforce the point, the dinghy then scraped on to solid tarmac where the road emerged above the surface of the water on the edge of the village itself.

Hauling the inflatable out of the water and, unbeknown to him, dumping it on the same patch of grass Kate had used just hours before, he looked for any sign of life, but through the dissipating mist saw only a narrow, empty street touched by tentative fingers of moonlight and bordered on either side by rows of cottages, with lights burning behind curtained windows. There was no other sign of anyone and the only sound that intruded on the still air was the relentless gurgle of water pouring from overfull gutters, even though the rain had now stopped.

Moving on, his torch in his hand, he passed the local inn, now shut up for the night and in total darkness, then the church, moonlight filtering through the thin skeins of mist to glitter on cold dark windows and touch tooth-like gravestones heeling over in the sodden earth as if silently mocking the holy ground in which they were embedded.

In spite of the adrenalin which relentlessly drove him on, he could not repress a shiver at these grim reminders of his own mortality or quell the fear dominating his thoughts that maybe he had arrived too late for Kate. Maybe – perish the thought – she had already been taken from him and was lying stiff and lifeless on a cold stone floor or in a tangle of undergrowth somewhere.

He clenched his free hand in an uncontrollable spasm in which both dread and a vengeful anger were equally mixed and it was then, just as he was about to press on past the church, that he heard something which stopped him in his tracks. It was the unmistakable bark of a firearm and it had come, he was sure, from within the very walls of that sacred place. Who on earth would be firing a gun inside a church? Swinging around, he pushed through the open gateway and headed for the building at a stumbling run.

Kate had deliberately avoided making for the hole in the wall that Lessing had used; she was pretty sure it was the first place Tommy would look. Instead, she left the yard via the archway Horse had earlier marched her through at the point of his pistol. She realized that the stone outhouse was a more difficult escape route, but felt sure that if, as Horse had claimed, Ellie Landy had made use of it, there was a very good chance she could do the same thing. It was one hell of a gamble, but then so was living.

There turned out to be no one lurking by the outhouse when she approached and, clambering on to the window sill, she was able to haul herself up on to the roof relatively easily. Several strands of wickedly sharp barbed wire ran along the top of the wall and they glinted in the moonlight as she peered over. About nine feet down, a rough track bordered the wall in both directions – to her left, cutting through woodland towards the gates of the house and the road in, and to her right, leading to heaven alone knew where. Directly below her, what looked like a leafless rowan tree sprouted from the foundations of the wall, reaching towards her like a three-fingered claw; her way out – if she didn't break her neck in the process.

Stripping off her anorak, she folded it to double its thickness and laid it over the wire, shivering as the cold damp air got to her bare flesh through her shredded blouse. Then, gingerly kneeling down on the wire, she tested the coat's resilience. Despite the thickness of the material, she felt the barbs pressing through her jeans into her knee. She grimaced, but re-positioned the anorak after folding it over on itself and tried again. Slightly better, but still dodgy. Then she saw the strip of denim cloth clinging to the wire just inches from her hand and remembered the injury to Ellie Landy's leg. Once again she thought, poor little Ellie had managed it, so why not her? It gave her all the incentive she needed.

'Thanks, Ellie,' she muttered and, gritting her teeth, held on to the wall over the folded anorak with both hands as she pivoted round on her right knee to face back towards the house and swung her left leg over the wall, feeling with the toe of her boot for a crook she had spotted in the top branch of the tree. She found it as one of the wire barbs cut into her knee through the anorak, making her cry out. She put all her weight on the branch, feeling it bend under her. Then, still gripping the wall with both hands, she raised herself up slightly to enable her to straighten her right leg sufficiently to slide it over the wall to join the left, ripping her jeans in the process and scrabbling for a few moments against the brickwork with her toe until she found another foothold on the branch which was now swaying and groaning alarmingly under her weight.

For several seconds she clung to the top of the wall with one hand as she worked at freeing her anorak from the grip of the barbed wire with the other, while trying to balance on the branch at the same time. She managed the feat in the end, tearing her hands as well as the coat in the process, but the branch had had enough and the next instant it gave up on her, snapping in two and pitching her into space.

A large shrub broke her fall, but she still hit the ground

heavily and lay among the remains of the bush for a couple of minutes, all the wind knocked out of her sails. But then a distant shout – seemingly from inside the grounds of the house – galvanized her into action and, hauling herself to her feet, she extricated herself with difficulty from the clutches of the branches in which she had become entangled and staggered to her feet to face the wall, bruised but not seriously hurt.

The track was like a white ribbon in the strengthening moonlight, still obscured in places by drifting patches of mist and stretching away on either side of her, following the line of the wall. It offered her a choice of direction and she was tempted to turn to what was now her left, deeper into the woodland, and find somewhere to hide, but she knew that that would be self-defeating. She couldn't stay hidden for ever and there was every chance Tommy and his thuggish companions would find her after a concerted search anyway. No, her only real option was to turn right, towards the main gate, and hope that she could get past it before anyone from the house came out – though what she did after that was anyone's guess.

Pulling on her torn anorak, she set off at a run, now painfully conscious of the lacerations to her hands and leg from the barbed wire and the bruises she had sustained to her back and rib cage in her fall. She was also close to exhaustion after all that she had been through. There was a persistent thudding pain in her head and her legs had developed an involuntary shake that slowed her up and affected both her muscular control and her ability to keep on a straight course. Twice she stumbled off the track into the shrubbery and once cannoned into the wall, badly grazing the back of her left hand.

But then she was off the track and on the approach road to the main gate of the house, the familiar voice in her brain urging her to 'run faster'. She heard a rumbling sound and, glancing over her shoulder, saw the gate to the house sliding open. The next instant she was spotlighted by the powerful beam of a torch and she heard someone yell out. Heavy footsteps rang on the surface of the road behind her, but she increased her pace, reaching the village main street well ahead of whoever was pursuing her. She glimpsed a narrow gap between two cottages on the other side of the road and, on impulse, sprang into it, crouching down in the shadows, panting heavily. Seconds later two figures, one a giant in a suit and the other shorter, thick-set and wearing a sweater, raced past, heading towards the church and the pub. Tommy and another man!

Then she heard a dog growl in the gloom behind her and caught sight of a pair of eyes studying her through a slatted gate. Damn it! If the dog started to bark, it would bring the two thugs racing back. And even as she thought about that, the animal released a couple of loud yelps.

She left her hiding place with another curse and stumbled across the street, looking for somewhere else to hide. But there was nowhere, just a terrace of cottages next to the passageway she had just left and, on the other side of the road, the village church with another terrace of cottages and the pub beyond.

The church – that was it! It was her best bet and there had to be all manner of nooks and crannies in such an ancient building where she could conceal herself.

She was through the gate into the graveyard moments before she heard heavy feet running back towards her from the direction of the pub. She made the shadows of the porch and froze as a giant figure stopped beside the gate and peered through into the graveyard. Tommy again, but alone this time; no doubt he had left his companion to check out the pub and other properties at the far end of the street.

Very carefully she raised the latch of the right-hand door and eased it open. To her relief it made hardly any sound.

Then she saw Tommy coming through the gate into the grave-yard, directing his torch into the clusters of gravestones. Holding her breath, she slipped sideways through the part-open door. Unlike Tommy, she had no torch – they had taken that from her at the house when she had been searched – but the moonlight stealing into the church through its stain-glass windows lightened some of the gloom and she was able to see enough to cross the stone floor to the far wall, resisting the urge to run. She probably had just a couple of minutes before Tommy finished checking the graveyard and actually came into the building. She had to find somewhere to hide before then or she was done for.

She saw the door to the sacristy and started towards it, then changed her mind. It was too obvious and from her knowledge of churches, she knew that there was unlikely to be anything in the room, save maybe a cupboard holding the sacred artefacts, a locker for the priest's robes and a chair. Absolutely nowhere to hide. Her eyes searched for the door to the tower, found it, but then dismissed that as well. She had no desire to play hide-and-seek with Tommy among the bells or end up trapped at the top of the tower until he found her and threw her off.

But then suddenly she had run out of time as the main door crashed back and Tommy stood there, framed in the opening, like some grotesque monster from the pages of mythology.

She just had the presence of mind to duck behind a row of pews a split second before the beam of his torch traced a line across the wall where she had been standing and then she heard his feet moving slowly towards her, grit on his leather-soled shoes scraping on the stone floor with each measured step.

'I know you're in here, bitch,' he said softly, 'and I'll find you, you can count on it, just like I found Ellie Landy.'

Her heart was making strange squishy noises and she

desperately tried to regulate her breathing and hold back the panicky gasps that were forming in her throat. She was also conscious of a painful cramp developing in her left leg and, doing her best to manage the pain, she gripped the shelf running along the back of the pew she was sheltering behind to stop herself losing her balance.

Silence. Tommy's feet were no longer scraping on the floor. He had stopped. Why? And where the hell had he gone?

The cramp in her leg was becoming unbearable and, to make matters worse, the shakes in both legs had now returned with a vengeance. She knew she couldn't remain in the same crouched position for much longer. She had to make a move.

Very carefully, she turned sideways and stretched out her left leg to flex it, gritting her teeth when the calf muscles knotted in an agonising spasm. As she waited for the spasm to pass, the shakes in her right leg – now bearing all her weight – produced a wobble at the knee, which she found difficult to control. Forced to try and change her crouched position completely, she lost her grip on the shelf of the pew she was hiding behind and cannoned into it with enough noise to wake every bat in the vaulted roof.

At once came the rapid clump of leather shoes on the stone floor as Tommy ran in the direction of the sound. Then the footsteps stopped and the beam of his torch passed over her head, probing the shadows at the far end of the church. She could hear his harsh breathing and guessed he was standing in the middle of the nave, which meant that there were just two rows of pews between the pair of them. If he decided to walk down the aisle from where she had ducked into the pew which was now sheltering her, he could not fail to see her. She needed to move to the other side of the church as quickly as she could.

Turning sideways again, she managed this time to change her crouched position and get down on her hands and knees, pausing for a few moments as Tommy's torch swung over her head for a second time, spotlighting something that had attracted his attention, before swinging back again. She heard him snarl in frustration, but he stayed where he was, obviously watching and listening.

She moved off very slowly, still on her hands and knees, heading in the direction of the porch doors and lifting her feet at each stage to prevent the toes of her boots scraping on the floor behind her.

'You wait till I get hold of you,' Tommy shouted. 'Then you'll be sorry.'

Kate gnawed her lip, trying not to be spooked into making a sudden noise by crawling any faster. Then she was at the end of the pew, peering out into the aisle and across to the porch doors. She hadn't heard the scrape of Tommy's shoes again and guessed he was still standing motionless on the other side of the pews, waiting for her to crack first and give her position away. She tensed, focusing on the porch doors. They were only around ten to twelve feet away. She felt sure she could be through the unbolted door ahead of Tommy in a couple of bounds, slamming it behind her and streaking out of the gate before he could even get his Neanderthal brain in gear – but what if she was wrong? She grimaced. Only one way to find out and she couldn't stay crouched in the pew for ever.

Raising herself up on her haunches like an Olympic runner at the starting block, she counted to three, then four, then five – and suddenly went for it, throwing herself at the porch doors with the desperation of a hunted animal in its last burst of energy.

She heard Tommy erupt behind her, but got there before he was even halfway across the church, throwing the unbolted door open, then abruptly slamming to a stop before the figure standing in the porch in front of her.

'Going somewhere?' the man in the sweater said quietly, the pistol in his hand levelled at her stomach. 'I don't think so.'

CHAPTER 20

TOMMY WAS GRINNING like a psychotic on a double dose of happy pills when he came up behind Kate and peered over her shoulder into her face. He had patched up his knife wound with a large square of sticking plaster, but it was still leaking and below the plaster his face and neck glistened in the moonlight as the blood continued to stream down his lower cheek and neck into the collar of his shirt. After such a nasty injury, any normal man would have been severely incapacitated – maybe even have passed out – but Tommy was no normal man and, as Kate's gaze involuntarily flicked sideways, drawn towards that bestial disfigured face by some kind of macabre fascination, she saw her own cruel lingering death reflected in his mad gloating eyes.

'You'd better get back to the house,' Tommy told the man in the sweater. 'Boss will want to know what's happening.'

'What about her?' the other queried.

Tommy laughed – an inane unhinged sound that made Kate's flesh crawl. 'You leave her to me,' he replied. 'I've got a real special treat for our lady cop.'

As 'Sweater' shrugged and turned around to head back down the path to the gate, Kate felt something hard – obviously a pistol of some sort – press into the base of her spine and Tommy bent close to her ear, blood from his leaking wound smearing her own face. 'Back inside,' he said. 'Any tricks and I'll put a nine millimetre round in your pretty little arse.'

Kate inwardly shuddered and, well aware of the damage that a nine millimetre shell would do to her at such close range, she obediently turned back into the church, allowing him to prod her forward towards the centre aisle.

'Turn left towards the altar,' he ordered and, as she complied, he laughed again. 'You could try saying a prayer while you're here,' he mocked, 'but it won't do you any good.'

She didn't answer, but kept walking through an opening in a carved wooden screen into what she knew to be the chancel. There were rows of choir stalls on either side and the brass cross on the altar in front of her glinted in a river of moonlight which was now streaming through the high rose window above it.

'Left again,' Tommy ordered, tapping her on the back of the neck none too gently with his pistol.

There was a small low-level door there that she hadn't noticed before and he reached past her with his free hand to open it. 'After you,' he mocked and directed the beam of his torch past her through the doorway.

Kate detected the smell of damp stonework and stagnant water as she ducked through the opening and she found herself on a steep stone staircase, curving to her left as it dropped away into an oppressive darkness. At once realization dawned and she felt her stomach tighten. The crypt; they were going down into the crypt – the very crypt where Ellie Landy had met her death! By a cruel irony, she was about to retrace the same final steps Ellie had taken before she was murdered. So Tommy had a sense of humour after all – but that of a sadistic psychopath – and she knew that this time only a miracle could prevent her suffering the same horrific fate as the hapless journalist.

Even as her mind wrestled with the terrifying prospect of her own imminent death, the staircase came to an end. She found herself staring into a large underground chamber, lit by moonlight, which penetrated what would otherwise have been a Stygian darkness through gratings in the floor of the church above. The low roof was supported in the centre by a row of stone pillars, stretching away into the gloom like those of an ancient cistern she had once visited in Turkey, and the lids of a number of stone sarcophagi were just visible close to the walls on each side – just visible because the place was flooded to a depth of at least two to three feet by still murky water, which swallowed up the lower steps of the staircase, preventing further progress.

Instinctively, she swung round to face her captor who had now stopped a few feet away from her higher up the staircase. He emitted a short humourless laugh, apparently guessing what was going through her mind. 'Yeah, bitch, you've got it, this is where Ellie Landy went for her last swim. As the boss said, she tried to hide down here, see, but no one can hide from good old Tommy.'

'So you held her down on these steps with her head under the water until she drowned,' Kate summarized bitterly. 'You're no better than an animal.'

He deliberately shone the torch in her face, temporarily blinding her.

'Should have been nicer to me then, shouldn't she?' he snarled, his inane mirth abruptly subsiding. 'Just like you should have been.'

Kate swallowed hard. 'Maybe I could be?' she blurted in a last ditch effort to delay the inevitable. 'But not down here.'

He snorted. 'Like the last time, you mean?' he sneered, lowering the torch and glaring at her. 'Don't give me that crap. Anyway, it'll be more fun just snuffing your lights out and, as this piece is fitted with a silencer, no one will hear a thing, so I can take my time.'

Kate felt for the step below the one on which she was standing and winced as cold water began dribbling into her boots through the zips.

'Where would you like the first round?' he sneered. 'The gut maybe? Or would you prefer a shoulder? I've got a full mag, so we can play for at least a few minutes. You up for that?'

'Shoot me and my colleagues will know it was murder,' she said, conscious of the tremble in her voice. 'They'll hunt you and your boss down, wherever you try to hide.'

'That sounds like a line from an old movie,' he sneered, 'and I'm really scared.'

He advanced a few more steps towards her, his torch blinding her again. She retreated even further, the water now over her ankles and almost lapping her calves. She could smell the dankness of the stonework and the unmistakable odour of decay.

Tommy laughed again. 'Thinking about going for a swim with your boots on?' he mocked. 'I wouldn't bother. You'll have so many holes in you from my Browning before you hit the water that you'll leak like a sieve.'

Kate heard him rack the pistol. 'Maybe I'll just put one between your tits and have done with it,' he said, then added harshly, 'So, bye-bye, bitch.'

The sound of the pistol was very loud in the confined space, bouncing off the walls in an ear-splitting echo, and Kate instinctively flinched, wondering in a detached sort of way how it could be so loud when the gun was fitted with a silencer. But the anticipated impact of the 9 mm round never came. Instead, Tommy's huge figure – backlit by a powerful beam issuing from a point much higher up the staircase – seemed to shudder as part of his skull disintegrated and the torch and the automatic pistol slipped from his nerveless fingers to clatter down the steps in front of him. Then, as if caught by a camera in slow motion, his legs buckled and he pitched head-first down the steps and into the water right in front of her, his face and shoulders submerged and his lower body draped over the last few visible steps like a broken mannequin.

For a moment Kate just stared down at his prostrate body in a state of shock. Then, slowly climbing back out of the water, she stepped gingerly, disbelievingly over his body, as if half-expecting him to suddenly reach out and grab her ankle. The light still blazed at her from halfway up the staircase and she shielded her eyes as she made her way towards it, her feet squelching inside her sodden boots.

Horse waited for her to reach him, the smell from the recently fired automatic pistol in his hand still hanging in the damp air. He lowered his torch a fraction as she stopped a few steps below him.

'Why did you do that?' she said quietly.

He grunted. 'It was a good job I did,' he replied. 'I guessed Tommy would find you and knew what he would do to you when he did after your surgery on his face, so I made a point of following him.'

'But why?'

He shrugged. 'Maybe because I'm not a murderer and I don't go in for the killing of innocent people anyway – especially other cops,' and he added, tongue in cheek, 'even if they are blundering swedes.'

She ignored the dig. 'What are you going to do now?'

He emitted a cynical laugh. 'Run, seems to be a good idea?'

'Where to?'

'Wherever the Sandman goes – he's already decided it's time to clear out of here.'

'What about the floods and all his merchandise?'

'Sometimes you have to cut your losses and he reckons this place is getting much too hot for us now.'

'Both good swimmers, are you?'

'He has a fast boat in one of the barns and a plane ready at a private airfield not too far from here.'

'And you're going to stay with him after what you've just done to his favourite thug?'

'No choice. He's my only ticket out of the country.'

'But he'll kill you when he finds out.'

'Hopefully I'll have split by then – world's a big place,' and he laughed. 'I might even find some rogue state that's looking to recruit bent coppers.'

'Give yourself up.'

He turned away from her. 'Yeah, right. British justice and all that? No thanks.'

Then his torch was abruptly extinguished and with a soft, 'Stay cool,' he was gone, leaving her to stumble weakly after him, her body still shaking from the shock of what she had just witnessed and her feet inside the waterlogged boots fast turning into ice-blocks.

The crypt door had been left half open and she pushed through the gap like someone in a trance, straightening in the aisle beyond and standing there for a few moments, swaying drunkenly in a brilliant patch of moonlight, bewildered and uncomprehending.

And it was there that Hayden found her when he burst through the porch doors with the force of an express train to catch her in his arms as she collapsed in front of him.

Gabriel Lessing had phoned for breakdown assistance on his backup mobile half an hour ago, but so far no one had turned up. He was still sitting behind the wheel of his Volvo where Hayden had left him – crouched down as low as possible in the strengthening moonlight to avoid being seen – when Roscoe materialized through the patchy mist in his battered Honda Civic, a police Ford Transit filled with uniformed officers close behind him. As they clambered out on to the road, Lessing regained his courage at the sight of all the uniforms and scrambled from his car.

'I want to make a complaint,' he exclaimed, buttonholing Roscoe. 'One of your detectives – a man called Lewis, I believe – assaulted me and threw my car keys into the water. I've been left stranded in this damned place ever since.'

Roscoe stared at him with open hostility, noting out of the corner of his eye people emerging curiously from the adjacent cottages, attracted by the sight of so many police. 'Mr Lessing, isn't it?' he growled, turning his back on them. 'What are you doing here?'

The agency man faltered, suddenly realizing he had dropped himself in it. 'I – I was following up a story.'

'What story?'

Lessing swallowed hard and tried to bluff it out. 'That's my affair,' he replied with a resurgence of indignation, faltering again when he saw a couple of fire service vehicles suddenly arrive, one pulling a trailer with a large rubber dinghy mounted on it.

'What's going on?' he said, changing the subject.

Roscoe produced a cigarette and lit up, but ignored the question and, as he watched the fire service personnel offloading the dinghy, he came out with another of his own. 'Why did Lewis throw your keys in the water, Mr Lessing? And where is he now?'

Lessing stared at him blankly, suddenly stumped for an answer.

To his surprise Roscoe prodded him hard in the chest with one finger. 'I know why he chucked your keys away, Lessing,' he said, now dropping any pretence of politeness, 'because he called me and told me how you had run out on Kate Lewis. You're in deep shit, my friend, and I suggest you get yourself a very good publicist before your mates in Fleet Street hear about this and tear you apart.'

Then, leaving the little man babbling incoherently, he followed half a dozen of his officers down to the flooded section of the main road where the dinghy had been eased into the water and climbed aboard.

As the outboard motor sprang into life and the dinghy surged away from the bank into the patchy moonlit mist, Lessing stared after it, sensing that, far from landing the scoop of his life, when this story broke, he would be lucky if he even had a news agency left to run.

Hayden settled Kate gently in an end pew, removed his Parka and slipped it over her shoulders, pulling it across her chest over her anorak as she shivered inside. Then he bent down beside her to stroke her hair and peer up anxiously into her face. 'You OK, old girl?' he said. 'Gordon Bennett, I thought I'd lost you.'

'I'll be fine, Hayd,' she whispered, then, forcing a grin, quipped wickedly, 'But what took you so long?'

He snorted, missing her feeble attempt at humour. 'Dashed red tape, old girl, that's what,' he replied, then massaged his jaw with one cupped hand. 'And when I finally got here, I ran into that Gittings feller hiding in the shadows. Blackguard decked me before I even knew he was there, then ran off like the weasel he is.'

She grabbed his wrist. 'He saved my life, Hayd,' she said, shuddering as she thought of Tommy's skull being blown apart, 'and there's a corpse in the crypt, which would have been me if he hadn't turned up.'

He gave a short laugh. 'I expect we'd find a few dead-uns down there anyway, old girl,' he replied, 'so one more won't make any difference.'

She drew in her breath sharply, her frustration evident. 'You have to listen to me,' she said. 'Horse killed one of the Sandman's thugs to save me. We've got to bring him in before the Sandman finds out or he's dead.'

Hayden shook his head. 'No time for that,' he said firmly. 'We've got to get you out of here to safety. I've already been through to Roscoe and the troops are on their way, so we must leave it to them now.'

She put her hands against his chest and tried to push him away. 'I can't,' she gasped, her natural stubbornness trying to re-assert itself in spite of her condition. 'I know the house and I am the only one who can ID the Sandman. I *have* to be there when they go in.'

He stayed put, his bulk preventing her getting up. 'You may be the sergeant here,' he said with uncharacteristic firmness, 'but I am your husband and I'm telling you, there is no way you are going back into that house and that's final. I'll give Roscoe another call and tell him where we are.'

She sank against the back of the pew, suddenly too exhausted to argue anymore. 'So what do you suggest we do in the meantime, Mr Masterful?' she said weakly. 'Say a prayer?'

He released a soft chuckle. 'No,' he replied, 'but we could always take a look in the vestry to see if there's any communion wine there worth sampling.'

CHAPTER 21

Roscoe was cock-a-hoop. 'Got most of 'em, anyway,' he exclaimed. 'HQ brought in an armed response team in the chopper just as we got to the house and we caught the whole lot napping. Not a shot fired.'

It was now ten hours since the raid on the house in Lowmoor and watery sunlight stole into the conference room at Highbridge police station through the grimy windows. The wash-up – or preliminary debrief – had been set up in advance of a reluctantly convened press conference and the mark of exhaustion was clearly written on most of the faces gathered around the long shiny table.

'Who exactly did we get, Guv?' Kate queried tightly.

Roscoe frowned and glanced at both Hart and Ricketts before turning back to her. The DI had been against Kate being there at all, seeing her as a potentially disruptive influence after her ordeal, and he would rather have seen her packed off home to rest – Hayden's view too. But she had insisted on attending the wash-up and Ricketts – showing his usual lack of empathy – had agreed.

'We nicked five of them,' Roscoe said awkwardly. 'Two known faces from the Smoke – low-life enforcers – and three rogue pharmacists still in their bloody white coats.'

'But no Sandman?' Kate persisted.

Another deeper frown. 'We found no one bearing the description you gave us, Kate,' the DI said, then added, exuberantly slamming his fist on the table, 'but we smashed the bloody gang, didn't we? And we've seized the biggest stash of illegal drugs the UK has ever seen, plus all the kit they've been using. Not bad for a night's work, eh?'

'But that still doesn't alter the fact that the Sandman got away,' Hart commented drily.

Roscoe grimaced, suddenly deflated. 'Yeah, it seems he had a dinghy of some sort in one of the barns and he and Gittings – and maybe another low-life scarpered in it across the flooded fields. The chopper lost them in the dark.'

'Well, they can't have got far. They must be on foot some-where out on the marsh?' Hart continued.

Roscoe shook his head gloomily. 'Just heard that a Traffic mobile has found an inflatable dumped in a gateway on some high ground above the flood level about two miles away and heavy tyre tracks leading out on to a drove that look like those made by a 4 x 4.'

'It may not be the same boat. There are loads of them in use around here at the moment,' Ricketts pointed out, running his long thin fingers through his thatch of blond hair.

'Yeah, but it's a bit of a coincidence, isn't it and it was a damned funny place to leave an inflatable.'

'Then Pavlović must have had access to a vehicle?' Kate put in again.

Roscoe nodded. 'Probably knew of some other local low-life he could call on his mobile to pick him and his crew up.'

'Which means this Pavlović character is free to start up somewhere else?' Ricketts commented with more than a trace of critical acid in his tone.

'We've put out an all-ports warning,' Roscoe snapped defensively, 'and Interpol will also be advized. Nothing more we can do at this stage.'

'What about the private airfield Horse told me about?' Kate asked.

'Checks are being carried out as we speak,' the uniformed chief inspector at the far end of the table put in. 'But there are several operational and allegedly disused strips in the south-west, so it could take a while.'

'By which time it will be too late – if it's not too late already?' Kate went on.

The chief inspector said nothing, but shrugged in helpless agreement.

'And on top of everything,' Hart added grimly, 'we now have a prat of an undercover copper who's got himself in the frame for murder.'

Kate's eyes smouldered. 'A prat who saved my life,' she said pointedly. 'The thug he shot was about to put a bullet in me. What else should Horse have done?'

Hart didn't answer and there were a few moments of embarrassed silence, which Roscoe broke with a character-istic grunt. 'That will be taken into consideration when we finally bring him in, Kate,' he reassured gruffly, kicking the issue in to touch, 'so let's leave it there for the moment, shall we?'

He turned away from her, his boot-button eyes darting from face to face. 'And I suggest we leave everything else as it is for now too. Forensic teams are already on site, together with the drug squad, and Mr Hart here is arranging for a team from the NCA to attend later this morning. The pathol-ogist and coroner's officer are at the church dealing with the bloody stiff in the crypt and we've taped off the church and the house and put a cordon in place. So there's nothing more we can do until the "woodentops" start making their routine house to house inquiries in a couple of hours.'

The uniformed chief inspector flushed at the uncomplimen-tary reference to his officers, but before he could cut Roscoe off at the knees, Hayden jumped to his feet with a wide grin. 'Then maybe we should get some lunch?' he said. 'My stomach feels as though my throat's been cut.'

Ricketts gave him an old-fashioned look, but nodded, shuffling a file of papers in front of him and also climbing to his feet. 'There will be a full debrief at 1500 hours,' he said. 'Chief Super and ACC, Territorial Policing, will be here then with the force press officer. I suggest we get our heads down for a few hours' kip in the meantime. It's going to be another long day.'

'Home then?' Hayden beamed at Kate, easing her chair out from the table so she could climb to her feet as the others filed out of the conference room. 'What's it to be? One egg or two?'

She shook her head with a sour grimace. 'You really are something else, aren't you?' she snapped.

'I know,' he said, totally unabashed. 'But that's why you married me, isn't it, sweetness?'

Kate abandoned her big double bed just four hours after climbing between the sheets. She had turned down Hayden's offer of lunch, but a hot shower had relaxed her to the point where sleep had come easily. Yet it hadn't lasted. A succession of horrific dreams, coupled with renewed pain from the lacerations and bruises she had sustained in her escape from the house in Lowmoor, had given her no peace and in the end, she had decided to get up two hours ahead of the main operational debrief that was due to take place at Highbridge police station at 1500 hours, leaving Hayden snoring away as his stomach digested the mammoth helping of sausage, bacon and eggs he had put away.

The phone rang as she was taking another shower and she ran naked and dripping into the bedroom to pick up the call on the extension as Hayden began to stir irritably.

'Hello, Sergeant Lewis,' the quiet voice said. 'I hope I didn't wake you after your ordeal.'

Kate stiffened. The voice was unmistakable; she would have recognized it anywhere. 'You've got a bloody nerve,' she exclaimed, feeling strangely vulnerable in her nakedness, despite the fact that the Serb was on the other end of a phone. 'How did you get my number?'

Pavlović laughed. 'Ah, now that would be telling, wouldn't it? Suffice it to say that the Sandman has very good intelligence on these things.'

Kate glared at Hayden, who had gone back to sleep, willing him to wake up, but he slept on with a big fat smile on his face.

'The thing is,' Pavlović continued, 'I was truly mortified that we didn't get time to say au revoir.'

Kate strained her ears. She could hear a sound in the background; a powerful engine turning over. The Serb was either in a car or close to one – no, it wasn't a car it was a helicopter, the distinctive thud of the rotor blades was unmistakable.

'Flying out now, are you?' she said.

Another laugh. 'What a clever girl you are, my dear – but no, just about to actually. Pilot is warming her up for us.'

'I thought a scumbag like you would be on your way to your next rat-hole long before now?'

Pavlović sighed heavily, seemingly taking her insults in his stride. 'So did I, my dear,' he replied,' but sadly, the weather was against us at first and then we had a spot of engine trouble – though all solved now.'

'So why the telephone call?'

Hayden suddenly sat bolt upright beside her, rubbing his eyes and looking bewildered. 'W-what?' he blurted, still half-asleep.

Kate waved him to silence.

'Thought I'd ring to say I've got a present for you,' Pavlović replied. 'Going to drop it in to you on my way out of the country.'

Kate's eyes narrowed. 'A present? What sort of present would that be?'

Another laugh. 'Oh, you know, just something to remember me by. Hope you like it. Ciao, as our Italian cousins would say.'

Then the line went dead.

'What the devil was all that about?' Hayden demanded, now fully awake and taking in her nudity with raised eyebrows and a hopeful gleam in his eyes, which was not reciprocated.

Instead, Kate treated him to a preoccupied frown as she replaced the phone, deeply disturbed by the call and apprehensive as to what the sadistic Serb might have in mind. 'That was Pavlović,' she said. 'He was in a chopper. Told me he had a present for me.'

Hayden's expression abruptly changed. 'A present? The cheek of the scoundrel,' he said hotly.

Kate gave a tight humourless smile. Good old Hayden – polite to the last.

'We'd better get dressed,' she said. 'I have a bad feeling about this.'

'I'll ring the nick,' he said, rolling across the bed to pick up the extension phone from its base. 'Get some backup here.'

'Backup for what?' she queried, as she reached for the clothes she had left folded neatly over the back of a nearby chair. 'We have no idea what he's planning.'

Hayden snorted, now also out of bed, but back on his own side, clad in his infamous boxers and a pair of grey socks. Stabbing the keys of the phone he was holding with the index finger of his other hand, he grimaced. 'Won't be a bottle of bubbly anyway,' he retorted. 'You can be sure of that—'

She waved him to silence and, darting across the room to the window, jerked the curtains back. 'Can you hear it?' she said.

He terminated the call before he had finished dialling and joined her at the window, his head cocked on one side to listen. He heard the sound of the engine immediately, accompanied by the rhythmic thud of rotor blades. 'A chopper,' he said as the sound increased in volume, 'and heading this way.'

'There!' Kate exclaimed and pointed.

The black dot grew rapidly as it sped towards them over the tops of the trees and hedgerows, taking on its distinctive shape within seconds, sunlight glittering on its bulbous windshield.

'Out!' Hayden yelled suddenly, grabbing his tartan dressing-gown from the bed and pushing her towards the door. 'It's coming straight for us!'

Kate just had time to grab her own white towelling robe from the back of the door before the helicopter's nose filled the window like the eye of some giant attacking bug, its deafening roar shaking the old cottage to its foundations.

But then, even as Kate struggled into her robe, Hayden was propelling her down the wooden staircase and out through the front door, gravel biting into the soles of their feet as they raced down the path and out through the front gate into the road, where a small knot of startled curious people from adjacent houses was already beginning to gather.

The anticipated explosion or rattle of a semi-automatic weapon never came, however, and, turning as the sound of the helicopter's engine note changed, they saw it lift high above the roof of the cottage and pause in hover mode over the driveway where Hayden's red Mk2 Jaguar was parked. Then, a side door opened and something long and black either fell or was thrown out before the machine lifted again and thudded away back across the fields towards Burnham-on-Sea and the coast.

'What the devil was that?' Hayden exclaimed, but Kate was already sprinting off barefoot along the pavement towards the side gate.

Hayden was only a yard or so behind her and he cannoned into her just inside the gateway, staring at the buckled roof of his Jag and the 'thing' that was lying on top of it.

That it was the body of a man was plain to see – the arms

and legs splayed over the edges of the roof like those of a broken doll and the head lolling back grotesquely over the rear window, blood streaming down the glass from what had to be some kind of horrendous wound to the back of the skull.

Even before she got to the car, Kate instinctively knew the identity of the dead man and, once there, her worst fears were confirmed. 'I've got a present for you…. Something to remember me by.' Pavlović's words echoed over and over again in her brain as she stared helplessly and with a sense of unutterable horror, into the vacant brown eyes and white bloodless face of the late Larry Gittings.

'According to Lydia Summers, Gittings was dead before he was thrown out of the helicopter,' Hayden said, dropping into the chair opposite Kate, who was slumped in a corner of the settee with a glass of brandy clasped in both hands.

She made a face and took a sip of her brandy. 'I saw the bullet hole in his forehead,' she said.

Hayden nodded. 'Nine millimetre the pathologist reckons and probably a hollow point round, going by the size of the exit wound to the back of his skull.'

Kate shuddered, not for the first time in the last twenty-four hours. 'Poor devil,' she muttered.

Hayden shrugged. 'He knew what he was getting into when he changed sides,' he pointed out. 'There was always the risk that he would end up on a mortuary slab.'

She flinched slightly at his insensitivity. 'Turncoat or not, he still didn't deserve to die like that.'

'In my book, no one deserves to die like that, old girl,' he replied. Then he frowned. 'Only thing I can't understand, though, is why Pavlović indulged in such a pointless charade when he could have simply dumped Gittings in a hole somewhere and bolted, with no one being the wiser?'

Kate set down her glass and drew her robe more tightly about her. 'It wasn't a pointless charade, Hayd,' she replied.

'Don't you see? He wanted to let us know that he had won – after all our efforts, he still got away.'

'He hardly won, Kate. As Roscoe said at the debrief, we smashed his organization and seized the biggest haul of illegal drugs the UK has ever seen. And don't forget, he had powerful international backers who must have invested one heck of a lot in his operation. They won't be at all pleased about what's happened.'

She sighed. 'So, what now?' she queried, draining her glass.

He stood up, taking it from her. 'Well, SOCO are now doing their stuff outside,' he replied, 'and when they've finished, the coroner has given the OK for the body to be moved. Maybe then I can take a look at the dent in the roof of my Jag before we head off for the final debrief at the nick.'

'And then?'

He smiled. 'And then, Sergeant, you and I are going away for a much needed break. I've already cleared it with Roscoe and, with his usual bonhomie, he said he would be glad to get rid of the pair of us for a fortnight.'

'A fortnight?' she exclaimed. 'Where the hell are we going for a fortnight?'

'I thought a nice cruise would do the trick.'

She straightened up on the settee. 'And what would we do stuck on a cruise for two whole weeks?'

He looked her up and down, his eyes twinkling. 'Oh, I reckon I could think of at least one thing to keep us occupied, can't you?' he said.

She shook her head, treating him to an old-fashioned look. 'And the Sandman? What do we do about him?'

'We forget him,' he said quietly. 'He's someone else's responsibility now.' Then, setting her glass down on the nearby coffee table, he knelt on the edge of the settee, took her in his arms and kissed her. 'It's over, Kate,' he said. 'In my capacity as your husband, I declare this case closed.'

AFTER THE FACT

The Bosnian war had left its mark on Belgrade and the unmistakable scars of the bloody conflict were still in evidence in parts of the ancient city, even after so many years. The derelict two-storey warehouse in the downtown backstreet bore those same scars and, though there were signs that some restoration work had been carried out, the will seemed to have evaporated over time. As a result, the derelict shell remained a gloomy forbidding place, scarcely touched by the grey daylight filtering through the broken skylights and only offering shelter for the occasional vagrant or the desperate junkie searching collapsed veins for a new spot in which to plunge his dirty syringe.

Zoran Pavlović was very tense, though he tried not to show it in the presence of the minder who had driven him in a hired car from the airport to this pre-arranged rendezvous. He had good reason to be tense too. His beloved Serbia – and Belgrade in particular – was a major player in the trafficking of illegal drugs between Asia and Western Europe and the city of Belgrade had spawned any number of rival Mafia clans involved in the criminal trade. His UK operation had been part of one in particular, one that was fast emerging as the most powerful clan in the country, and the 'godfather' he was here to meet controlled an extensive network that had worldwide connections. If anyone could help him get back on his feet, it was Goran Jovanović, known as 'Snake Eye', but the wizened old man with the gaze of a cobra, who insisted on being called Father, would need convincing that Pavlović was worth a second chance – and that was what worried the albino, for he knew that Jovanović was not known for his forgiving nature and the old man had already invested a fortune in the now-aborted UK operation.

'Boss?' the thug in the driving seat said suddenly. 'We got company.'

Pavlović felt his stomach muscles tighten. The cavalcade consisted of four cars – all black Mercedes, all with headlights blazing, as they swept in through the gaping hole that had once accommodated big steel doors, swinging round in an untidy formation to face towards the exit again and skidding to a stop a few yards in front of Pavlović's car, transfixing it with their headlights.

For a moment there was no movement and then the front passenger door of one of the cars was thrown open in obvious invitation.

Pavlović touched his minder on the shoulder. 'Be ready, Kenny,' he said, 'just in case I need to get out of here in a hurry.'

The other grinned and tapped the Uzi on his lap. 'You bet,' he said.

Snake Eye was sitting in the back right-hand corner of the end Mercedes, slumped there, motionless, the single watery eye which had given him his nickname studying Pavlović through a film of mucus as he climbed into the front seat. The bald-headed Albanian who accompanied the Mafia godfather everywhere occupied the other rear seat beside his boss, but stared ahead without even acknowledging Pavlović's presence.

The albino forced a smile and turned in his seat to speak to the old man, but before he could say anything, Snake Eye spoke to him in a crackling voice like dry twigs rustling in a breeze. 'Face the front, Zoran,' he said in their mother tongue.

'We don't need to look at each other to talk.'

Pavlović glanced sideways at the driver but, like the Albanian, he remained impassive. 'There has been a problem with the UK operation, Father,' he said.

There was a heavy sigh. 'That has already come to my notice, my son,' Snake Eye said, 'and I am very disappointed by the loss of such a profitable enterprise, but such things happen and we must put it behind us.'

Pavlović breathed a sigh of relief; things were going better than he had expected. 'Thank you, Father,' he said, 'I am only sorry I let you down and I will make it up to you in the future. I just need to lie low for a while, until—'

Then he broke off, stiffening in his seat. A dark figure in some sort of long coat had emerged suddenly from the shadows at the rear of the car he had hired from the airport and was approaching the driver's door. The next instant the figure appeared to raise an arm towards the window. There was a bright flash, but no sound and, even as it dawned on Pavlović that his minder had just been shot with a silenced pistol, the continuous blast of the car's horn as the dead man fell against the steering wheel was the last thing he heard.

The garrotte was applied with expert proficiency by the Albanian sitting behind him in the back seat, cutting off his air supply before he realized what was happening, and a bloody froth began to trickle from the corners of his gaping mouth as he writhed in the seat, clawing futilely at the thin cord biting into his neck.

Death came slowly, but surely and only when he ceased struggling altogether, his throat producing a long expiring rattle and his body relaxing and hanging limply in the improvised noose, did the Albanian slacken his grip and release the garrotte. Then, climbing out of the car, the killer calmly opened the front passenger door and hauled Pavlović's body out before carting it over one shoulder to the hire car and dumping it in the back seat behind the dead man slumped over the wheel.

The oily rag thrust into the petrol filler pipe was a simple expedient and the brief flash of a match preceded an even brighter flame. The four car cavalcade was already pulling away when the Albanian jumped into the second Mercedes beside Jovanović and, as they raced out of the warehouse on to the road, the violent explosion in the gloom behind them lit up the interior of their vehicle almost with the brilliance of an exploding star.

'Your father forgives you, Zoran,' Snake Eye murmured in his crackly voice, as he studied the leaping flames in the driver's rear view mirror, 'but, sadly, forgiveness is never enough.'